LOCKDOWN

HORROR #2

Compiled & Edited by

D. Kershaw | Maggie Pawsey | S.N. Graves

Also available and coming soon from Black Hare Press

DARK DRABBLES ANTHOLOGIES

WORLDS

ANGELS

MONSTERS

BEYOND

UNRAVEL

APOCALYPSE

LOVE

HATE

OCEANS

ANCIENTS

BHP WRITERS' GROUP SPECIAL EDITIONS

STORMING AREA 51

EERIE CHRISTMAS

BAD ROMANCE

TWENTY TWENTY

OTHER VOLUMES

DEEP SPACE

WHAT IF?

KEY TO THE KINGDOM

DEEP SEA

BEYOND THE REALM

Twitter: @BlackHarePress

Facebook: BlackHarePress

Website: www.BlackHarePress.com

Cover design	Dawn Burdett	www.dmburdett.com
Formatting	Ben Thomas	www.blackharepress.com
Editing	D. Kershaw	www.blackharepress.com
	Maggie Pawsey	
	S.N. Graves	www.sngraves.com
Read Team	David Green	davidgreenwritercom.wordpress.com
	Jennifer Hatfield	jhatfieldauthor.wixsite.com/website
	Jodi Jensen	jodijensenwrites.wordpress.com
	Lyndsay Ellis-Holloway	authorlyndseyellisholloway.webador.co.uk
	Stacey Jaine McIntosh	www.staceyjainemcintosh.com

TABLE OF CONTENTS

THE FACE IN THE FABRIC

By Tim Mendees

"Fantasy, abandoned by reason, produces impossible monsters; united with

it, she is the mother of the arts and the origin   of   marvels. "
— Francisco de Goya

Have you ever seen faces in fabric?

Do you sometimes find yourself staring at a crumpled towel or bedsheet? Are your eyes drawn to curtains or washing flailing on the line? Sometimes, do you begin to see forms taking shape? Do these faces inspire you? Do they chill your soul?

If the answer is yes, then let this document of my undoing serve as a dire warning...

***

My name is Frank Blake, an artist and

wood sculptor of renown. My specialities lie in the dark and grotesque. I strive to bring life to the pieces I create. No matter how disturbing that life may be. For what is art without life?

My creations have delighted and repulsed in equal measure. After embarking on my chosen path, I quickly garnered acclaim and accolades. But as all good things must end, so did my run of good fortune. I had found myself struggling for over a year to create anything more than mere crones-by numbers and other cliché-ridden pieces unworthy of my name.

By the beginning of the year, my finances were in a dire state, and I was in danger of losing my barn-conversion home in the isolated wilds of Cornwall. The red letters were beginning to stack up, and my creditors were beginning to get restless. It would not have been long before the bailiffs came knocking.

Salvation came in the surprising form of a small, unappealing man named Arthur. He and a small consortium had recently purchased Barncoose Manor. An old stately pile situated just over a mile away from my studio, near the small village of High Bend. They planned to restore the manor to its former glories and turn it into an attraction of sorts.

Escape rooms had become the flavour of the month of late, offering interactive theatre, brain-taxing puzzles and a dash of the Grand Guignol to thrill-seekers and amateur sleuths alike. Arthur was already familiar with my work and had been impressed by the grotesque nature of my oeuvre. He appeared on my doorstep one day in March and offered me a *very* handsome sum to create some bespoke sculptures for display in their enterprise.

Art, as he preferred to be known, was a strangely revolting little man with a distinctly toad-like appearance. He was the living embodiment of the term, slimy. Over a drink, Art explained at length what he desired me to create. I sat in uneasy fascination as I watched his thick, fleshy lips go up and down, his tongue slurping disgustingly. He wanted me to complete three sculptured portraits of a horrific and fantastic nature. I was given free rein over two of the three pieces. The third piece was to be an active part of the escape room experience and as a consequence, I would have to work to design.

The full details of the third piece would be revealed to me nearer the completion date six months hence. They would take this extended period to work out exactly what they needed for their puzzle. Iron out the kinks, so to speak. I readily agreed to the offer and ordered the wood accordingly.

I had chosen my abode due to its blissful isolation and distance from *civilisation*. I have never been what you could call a sociable creature, and I much prefer my own company over the cattle of the towns and cities. Here I could hone my craft in peace and seclusion. Enduring none of the toe-curling interruptions or distractions that plagued my previous, city-based, studio.

The quiet solitude that my self-imposed exile provided was an essential part of my creative process. Only when my mind is clear of all outside agencies, can I conjure the images I need to transfer lifeless lumps of wood into a state of eternal life.

This probably sounds like the sort of nonsensical gumpf that *artists* have spouted for millennia, but I know the truth of my statement. I have seen—and yes, have created—life through art. I have spoken to the things that dwell in the mediums of the gifted and have suffered terribly as a consequence. Leading me inexorably towards the drastic actions that I must now take...

Alas, I am getting ahead of myself. Upon the arrival of the wood, I set about preparation of the surfaces, sanding down the edges to ensure that they were smooth and perfectly circular.

As per my commission, I purchased three consecutive intersections of the same tree trunk. At a great personal cost, I might add. Each slice was of equal diameter and thickness, thirteen inches deep. This would allow me plenty of room to create a striking 3D image on each piece.

The way I usually work is thus: I begin by stretching a very thin piece of cloth over the surface then, using a stick of charcoal, I create the lines of the visage or scene following the grain and natural contours of the wood. Once I have a clear idea of the image I intend to create, then I can move on to the carving, sanding, shaping and finally, varnishing of the wood.

As I mentioned earlier, I had been struggling with a dearth of inspiration of late. The gift of free rein over a piece is usually a great boon to an artist such as I, but at that moment in time, it felt more like a curse. For days and weeks, I stared at that first hunk of wood. I cannot even begin to guess at how many reams of fabric I ruined. The mistakes were unceremoniously balled-up and thrown in the corner of my studio where they grew into a towering monument to my failure.

More than a month passed, and I was

no nearer completion than when I started. Desperation and anxiety had ballooned in my guts to a colossal size. My GP prescribed some powerful antidepressants and tranquillizers to soothe my screaming soul, but none of his pills and potions could aid my art.

No matter what I did, I just couldn't decide on a picture. I had grown so damn tired of the usual grotesque tropes—the staring-eyed crooked old man, the hatchet-faced old crone—I wanted to create something new. Something memorable. Something worthy of my name, and the money I had been promised...

***

For many years before this time, I had struggled with drink and drug abuse and had suffered through more than one spell in rehab. The intense frustration of my artist's block had driven me to breaking point, and I sought solace in the bottle once more. The longer I couldn't work, the drunker I became and the drunker I became, the less likely it was that I would be able to work. It was a vicious circle of such appetites that it seemed I was destined to be devoured by it.

During one particularly ferocious stupor, I unleashed the fury of my carving tools on a thin dividing wall, slicing my hand open in the process. When I awoke the following morning to the rank, metallic smell of my own blood, I sank even lower. I used some of the discarded fabric to scrub the blood off the walls, then returned the bloodied items to the pile in the corner and bandaged my hand.

I spent the next couple of days in a state of acute sedation. I gobbled up my pills like a good little boy, exceeding the prescribed dose by quite some margin. This at least meant I finally got some tortured sleep as I had been recently suffering through one of my frequent bouts of insomnia. I must have spent days dazed and confused, then, finally, inspiration came from an unusual place.

Under the effects of Diazepam and Scotch whiskey, I sat fuzzy-headed on the throne. The ceiling-mounted spot-lights were casting thick, gloomy shadows across the floor. I just sat there staring at nothing and everything and at some point my eyes came to settle upon the large beach towel that lay crumpled in the corner.

The dim yellow light hit the fabric at such an angle that great shadows and highlights were cast. As I sat for what seemed like an eternity, staring at my towel, faces began to appear. The optical illusion created by the folds in the towel and the angle of the light was amazing. Spellbinding. Various misshapen and deformed faces seemed to leer at me from the fabric, giving me chills.

After a while, all the faces seemed to blur into one monstrous whole. The face that grimaced at me from the soft material made me gasp in horror. The face was aquatic in design but neither ichthyic nor batrachian. Instead, it was a hybrid of both with a definite human aspect—as though it was spawned through an unholy union betwixt man, fish, and frog. A row of sharp pointed teeth lined the wide, fleshy mouth. The form was completed by a pair of hideously bulging eyes, scales, and the distinct suggestion of gills around the neck.

I knew in an instant that this was to be my first design. So, with a stub of a pencil that I keep in my pocket, I sketched the image onto a flattened toilet-roll tube then leapt into action.

For days I toiled, sanding, forming, shaping, until the terrible face from the cloth was transferred to the wooden circle. I knew the piece was good because it scared the bejesus out of me. Wherever I went, the bulbous, glassy eyes seemed to follow, the toothy grin smirking maliciously.

Upon completion of the first piece, a wave of relief washed over me. It was truly grotesque and seemed to exude a strange malevolence. The day after completion I called Arthur to give him the good news. He answered the phone in his customary slobbering manner; even down the phone he made my flesh crawl. I detailed the design and to my satisfaction, Arthur seemed more than just pleased. "Perfect, perfect" he kept repeating as I rambled on; he sounded excited, ecstatic even. I could picture his bulbous eyes twinkling with delight.

My elation upon completion of the first piece was short-lived, however. As before, I had no inkling as to what to produce for the second. I ruminated over the design until after another night of heavy drinking I sat hungover on the throne once again. I pulled the towel onto the floor and after ages of staring at various little furtive faces, inspiration loomed once more. The face was of a similar breed as before, only this one was possessed of a distinctly feminine aspect complete with pendulous, scaly breasts.

I swiftly copied the outlines of the fabric form with the only things I could lay my hands on. Using an old razorblade, I scratched the design into a piece of skirting board that I yanked off the wall. I also cut my fingers to ribbons in the process. You have to suffer for your art, after all, for what is art without suffering?

The piece developed quickly, and upon completion was just as hideous as the first. If anything, this sculpture was more unsettling than the other, as it harboured a strange kind of allure. The breasts drooped obscenely, and the wide mouth was twisted into something akin to a seductive smile. Again, the eyes seemed to study my every movement with malignant interest. The feeling of being watched became so strong that I was forced to cover both sculptures with a blood-stained bedsheet.

I was happy with my work and convinced that I had earned my commission. There was a week to go before the deadline where I would receive specifics on the final sculpture, so I decided to celebrate in style. Firstly, I ordered some fine wines and cigars from the nearby town then scored some amphetamines from my local source.

I made a half-hearted attempt at cleaning up the studio as it was in a terrible state. I always make a mess when I work but this time was special. Amongst the sawdust, shavings and other wood debris were a mountainous collection of empty bottles, cigarette boxes and dog-ends, pizza boxes, and the enormous pile of blood and charcoal stained fabric.

For three days and nights, I revelled. I drank, snorted, and smoked until my body collapsed from the exertion, and I passed out on the studio floor. I have the vaguest recollection of awakening at some point, face to face with absolute horror. I was lying on the floor with my head facing the pile of discarded fabric. This time there was no delay between staring and the image materialising.

The image was of a bulbous head with blank, staring eyes. It was the rest of the face that was the worst, however. Huge writhing tentacles spread from under the eyes. The loops and folds of the fabric, shaded with charcoal and blood, gave it an unnatural life. I remember thinking that I needed to get the image copied, then all went black...

***

When I finally awoke from my stupor,

it was to a nightmare. Next to my prone body was a scalpel, a bloody cloth, and a fragment of the mirror I had put my fist through in frustration weeks before. The copper and iron smell of dried blood assaulted my sinuses, and my chest was sticky and painful.

I had carved the image from the fabric on my chest using the mirror as a guide, then pressed the cloth on the wound. Transferring the image in a similar way to woodcut printing or what children do with potatoes and poster paint.

My chest hair was matted in globs of sticky, dried blood and the wound stung like hell. I grabbed some more of the fabric and tried to wipe away some of the clots. My fingers were a mess again, and as I sat up, I noticed a trail of red towards my workbench.

Panic seized my heart in a vice-like grip when I eyed the workbench. The last precious slice of wood had been carved. The monstrous face from the fabric stared back at me from the workbench, looking hungry. I stared in horror as the tentacles seemed to squirm and writhe and the eyes seemed to burn like hot coals. I was entranced by the horrific sculpture and only a sharp rapping at the door broke its spell.

I quickly searched out and wore a black T-shirt to hide the bloodstains. Deep desperation gripped me as I opened the door to find the misshapen form of Arthur standing in the rain. I honestly feared that I had blown the contract by defacing the brother piece of wood to the others. I begrudgingly opened the door wider and let him in.

Arthur didn't seem at all taken aback by the state of the studio and either didn't see or care about the bloodstains on the walls and floor. His manner made me a trifle uncomfortable as he eyed the two aquatic sculptures with a sort of manic glee. He kept muttering "Perfect" to himself again as he wiped sweat and rainwater off his balding pate with a piece of discarded cloth. Once he had enthused about the two works, I decided that then was the best time to own up to my mistake.

I explained what had occurred, then begged and pleaded with him not to cancel the commission. Vowing that I could, and would, find an almost identical slice of oak. After a few painful minutes of grovelling, I got the distinct impression that Arthur wasn't listening. He was transfixed on the carving of the tentacled creature.

After what felt like an age, he stuffed an envelope full of cash, more than initially agreed upon, in my bloodied hand. He commended me on a splendid job and explained that the third piece was perfect for their designs. After thanking me profusely, he gathered up the finished sculptures and left. A wide smile on his face.

I was elated. Confused, but elated, and after showering and dressing my wounds, I went to bed for a well-earned rest.

***

I slept for what must have been days. All the while I was haunted by that monstrous face from the fabric. It came to me across vast oceanic vistas of sunken cities and basalt monoliths. It spoke of the father and the mother and their exile beneath the surface. The god, for that is what the terrible being is, talked of returning to the surface when the stars were right, and that I had a crucial part to play in the coming maelstrom of insanity and terror. I begged to be released from my bond and pleaded with it to be left alone. The sound of its laughter now haunts my every moment.

When finally I awoke from my

tortuous slumber, it was to one of my many creditors banging on the door. I arose and paid the man with notes from the envelope. As he went away happy, I discovered a sheet of A4 paper tucked in with the cash.

My head spun with a colossal shock when I unfolded the proposed design for the third piece. There on the page, in amateurish chicken scratches, was a drawing. The design was almost identical in almost every way to the aquatic horror I had immortalised in oak.

From that moment on, I have had no peace, no respite. Whenever I look at anything made of fabric, I see the horror. When I draw the curtains or make the bed, there it is, lurking. In a wild frenzy, I tore down the curtains and burned them along with anything else made of fabric. Excepting my clothes, of course. But still, the nightmares came. Still, the horror spoke to me, trying to cajole me into doing its bidding. The more I refused, the worse the visions became.

Finally, I decided that my clothes must be incinerated to erase all traces of fabric from the house. I was hopeful that it would be enough to rid myself of this entity. Sadly, I was wrong.

I screamed in anguish as I stared into the bathroom mirror at the horrific face that stared back at me from the very fabric of my skin. I smashed it in despair and have been locked in my bare studio for almost a week now. The dreams still haunt me, however, and it has become clear that there is only one course of action to take. There is no other way to rid myself of the creature's insidious influence...

I have sharpened my carving tools in preparation for what must be done...

***

Please find attached the final written notes on the alleged suicide of Mr Frank Blake.

Dear Inspector Baker,

I have completed the preliminary psychiatric assessment in relation to the case of Frank Blake. It is of my professional opinion that Mr Blake was suffering from paranoid delusions and possible schizophrenia. The phenomena of seeing faces in objects is often a symptom shared by paranoid schizophrenics.

Mr Blake has a long history of depression and violent outbursts. He had twice before been committed to mental institutions for dissociative episodes but was released as cured. Along with the suspected schizophrenia, Mr Blake has shown evidence of various personality disorders, such as histrionic, grandiosity, narcissistic, and persecution.

From the medical report, I notice that the cause of death was from massive blood loss, caused when Mr Blake nicked an artery while trying to remove 'the face' from his chest by effectively skinning himself. This was obviously brought on by hallucinations and the substance abuse that he had relapsed into.

I am confident to give the opinion that Mr Blake was insane at the time of taking his own life and hereby release the body to his relations.

Yours Sincerely.
Imogen Thwaite. MD.
Betyls Cove Hospital.

P.S. If you manage to track down this 'Arthur' let me know. I am interested in viewing Mr Blake's work. Though, as we discussed, I'm almost sure that the man is merely another delusion.

THE SEED

By McKenzie Richardson

It was raining when she found it. That's why she'd noticed it in the first place. Its crimson colour was so at odds with the dreary surroundings, it was impossible to miss.

She couldn't say why she picked it up. Curiosity, most likely. She tapped her phone and examined the thing in its pale light.

It was about the size of a golf ball and fit perfectly in the palm of her hand. Its ruby surface shimmered slightly in the light, oddly beautiful.

She decided to take it home.

That night, she searched online, trying to identify the thing. Its slight asymmetry gave it an organic look. A bulb? A pit?

She stumbled across images of avocado seeds. Besides the colour, it bore a striking resemblance. The oblong shape, the smoothness. It was probably some weird strain. Maybe she could grow her own tree that bore red fruit.

LOCKDOWN HORROR #2

As the internet advised, she stabbed in a few toothpicks. Minuscule drops of scarlet liquid seeped out as she did. She placed it in a jar of water, the toothpicks supporting it so it rested just at the water's surface.

She set it near the window, so it would get plenty of sun.

And then she waited.

Nothing happened the first week.

Or the second week.

Or the third.

During the fourth, she had just herself resigned to throwing the thing out when she noticed the change. There was a crack in it, just at the bottom where it touched the red-tinged water.

She examined it more closely. The

crack was large enough to peek inside, and when she did, she saw the end of a pale taproot, the colour of starlight, starting to poke its way out.

She gawked in wonder, then set it back in the water.

For the rest of the week, the thing grew and grew, a little bit more each day. The dark outer covering had gone midnight blackish and soon flaked off, revealing a bright red interior that gleamed like fresh blood.

She supposed it wasn't really a "thing" anymore and decided to start thinking of it as a seed, the growth finally confirming her suspicions.

She watched it grow, the taproot slowly inching its way out.

LOCKDOWN HORROR #2

When the root was three inches long, she relocated it to a bigger jar. The next week, she had to move it to an even larger one. It seemed the more space the seed had, the more inclined it was to grow.

She put it in the deepest jar she could find—a massive pickle jar from the very back of the cupboard. Inside this jar, the thick taproot branched off into smaller roots that spread across the bottom like pale veins. They formed little squiggly tails, snaking their way up the sides until they filled most of the space.

She knew she'd have to find a deeper jar soon. She shrugged, putting it off for another day, and prepared for bed.

It rained that night, a comforting drizzle that sent a sense of calm through her mind. To enjoy the freshness of the air, she left the window open just a crack. She fell asleep to the lullaby of the pitter-patter on the windowpane.

Sometime past midnight, the smell of dampness woke her. It wasn't the usual smell of rain. It was earthlier and more humid, like being encased in a greenhouse. She swung her legs off the bed to close the window.

As she stood, she was overcome with light-headedness. She clasped the window frame to keep her balance. Once the wooziness had passed, she chastised herself for getting up too fast, shut the window, and went back to bed.

Beneath her feet, the floor was slightly wet. The rain must have been stronger than she'd thought. She'd clean it up in the morning.

As she flopped back onto the bed, she felt a heaviness on her chest. She put her hand to it. There she felt something long and wet and smooth. Slightly dreamily, she followed one end which led her fingers to a hole in her shirt. Something snake-like rested against her skin, slightly sticky.

She flipped on the bedside light, then screamed, fear shocking her fully awake.

From her chest sprouted a protrusion as thick as her wrist and the colour of starlight. She stared at it, horrified, then trailed the other end with her eyes. It was connected to many more star-coloured branches, like ropes or vines or—

*Root*s.

In that moment, everything clicked in her mind like the last piece of a puzzle, the true horror of the ordeal setting in.

She could feel the root pulsing in her chest, gorging on her blood. Vomit rose in her throat and erupted onto the bedsheets.

She grabbed the root with both hands to yank it from her, but an agonizing tightness in her chest made her stop. It felt as though she were pulling out her own heart. Perhaps she was.

Images of the snaggle of roots exploring her organs filled her head and she fell back, feeling sick. Her vision blurred as she reached for her phone on the bedside table. In her search, she clumsily knocked over the bedside lamp, which shattered on the floor.

LOCKDOWN HORROR #2

She vomited again, her head spinning.

Her phone fell from inept fingers as the dizziness of blood loss disoriented her further.

Then, thankfully, she lost consciousness and didn't feel a thing. She wasn't scared or pained or horrified. She was just there, existing. Until she wasn't anymore.

The plant had wanted a bigger jar. And it had found one.

EYES FOR YOU

By K.B. Elijah

The girl followed her father into the greenhouse, exchanging the heady smell of manure for the delicate scents of lavender and thyme. The air was hotter in here too, the blazing sun amplified through the worn glass panes, despite it only having risen an hour ago.

She didn't like it in here, with its cramped aisles and uneven floor, and the ferns that brushed tauntingly against her bare arms.

She used to love this place. Back when it was just herbs and flowers, just her and her dad, it was a place of magic. A bubble of warm serenity sealed away from the world, shielded from her mum's episodes and her teachers' sighs. Their piece of paradise. She didn't mind the ferns then, because she knew what they were.

Just leaves seeking sunlight and water, harmless.

Now, when something touched her in here, she couldn't be assured of its intentions. She'd taken to wearing long sleeves despite the heat, sweat trickling down her back and forehead.

"Come," her father said impatiently, and she reluctantly increased her pace, scuffing her boots into thick piles of soil and rotting foliage, which released breaths of earthy scents into the air.

She knew where he was going. Before, he would have wandered the aisles of the greenhouse for hours, lingering fondly on one flower or vegetable before darting to the next. Now most of the plants were dead or dying, and he only had eyes for one.

Swallowing, she moved just close enough that he wouldn't snap at her for dawdling, but far enough away that she wouldn't accidentally brush against *it*.

She didn't like its feel: not cool, like most plants, but not hot either. A middling warmth that felt like flesh, slightly sticky and squishy under her fingers. The way it leaned into her touch, pressing against her skin more firmly than she was pushing back.

She remembered that sensation well as it had seared itself into her memory despite only having touched it once. She would not make that mistake a second time.

"Good morning, pretty," her father cooed, his voice as nauseatingly gooey as the plant itself. He never talked like that: not to her, not to her mum, not even to the foals he helped birth in the barn. Just to *it*.

"You are looking gorgeous today, if I may say so. And you're twice the size of yesterday!"

She took a small step backwards, hoping he wouldn't see the movement.

He didn't. He only had eyes for the plant.

"We are going to change the world, you and me. The wonders you bring! Indescribable colours, miraculous growth and healing abilities, your unbelievable reactions to external stimuli. They will *revere* us!"

He talked like this more and more these days, a crazed fervour in his words that scared her. Of course the plant was incredible: with what they had gifted it, how could it not be? But did he really think he would be credited with its find?

Even at eight years old, limited as she

was, she knew enough of the world to be certain that nothing ever worked out as planned. That was life, harsh and cruel.

"Let's see how yesterday's dinner worked out, shall we?"

She felt bile rise in her throat and stamped down the memory of feeding that thing the slimy handful of—

"What's..." Her father's voice faded to monosyllabic whispers of awe. "Oh. Wow. That's... W*ow*."

She couldn't help her curiosity. "Father? What is it?"

"It's beautiful," he breathed. "So beautiful. I need to...touch it..."

"Father!" she cried, reaching out for his arm but finding only air beneath her fingers. "We agreed to use gloves!"

LOCKDOWN HORROR #2

"Don't be silly," he said. "It won't *hurt* me. It just wants to—"

And then he screamed, a hollow shriek that cut through her bones like a shard of obsidian, slicing the very air around her. She smelled the tang of iron and knew he was bleeding.

They should never have fed it.

They shouldn't have noticed how it spurned ordinary plant food, shouldn't have experimented with raw cuts of beef and chicken. Shouldn't have listened as it slid slippery thoughts into their minds about what it would do with something more. They certainly shouldn't have given in to it, feeding it a toe, and then the foot, of the woman they found dead in their kitchen.

"It's what she would have wanted," her father had said eagerly, heaving the body into the chest freezer. "Your mum always felt so useless in life. She would be happy to be able to help in any way she could."

"Run!" the same man shouted now, his voice gurgling with effort, and she felt droplets of hot warmth land on her skin. "Don't let it—"

His plea was cut off with a sharp snap and a hideous slurping sound.

She backed away in horror, her heel smashing into a pile of broken plant pots.

If they hadn't fed it her mother's brain yesterday, there would have been no question about what would happen next. But they both had brains now, the girl and it. There was a battle of wits between them, where survival was the sought-after prize. It knew that if she escaped the greenhouse, she would not let it live. And if she didn't...

Maybe she could have. She was a smart eight-year-old after all, exasperating her teachers and confounding her fellow students. But since two weeks ago, when it had noisily consumed a slimy dinner, the plant had one thing she never had.

And that gave it the advantage.

For it had eyes.

DONE JUST RIGHT

By Gabriella Balcom

Thaddeus perked up, seeing Tantastic Tanning's "AMAZING DEAL" sign, and he relaxed in a tanning bed within minutes.

"It's getting hot," he soon called out, but nobody answered. When he pushed on the lid, it wouldn't budge, and he began pounding on it with his fists.

"All the beds are full," one tanning attendant told the other, locking the front door.

They morphed, eyes gleaming red in misshapen faces. Saliva dripped from their fangs.

"First order complete?" the second demanded.

"Yes. Well-done with a hint of charring."

"Good. The customers are hungry. Two medium-rares next."

First published *World of Myth Magazine*, 2019

DEATH BECOMES HER

By Cindar Harrell

The storm was picking up faster than I could wrap my mind around. What was going on? The winds shoved me in the open field, and the rain lashed my bare skin. The tattered black dress I wore served as little protection against nature's fury.

This wasn't supposed to happen!

How had an evening with friends gone so horribly wrong? The clash of metal on metal spurred me into action. I ran through the cornfield, trying to map out a course in my mind of the large property that might ensure survival. I needed shelter. The farmhouse was at the other end of the property, far out of reach, and the windmill was back the way I came.

That only leaves the barn. Perfect.

I paused at the cornfield's edge, hesitant to run out with such little cover, but the barn was in sight. I looked behind me.

All seemed calm. I ran for a large tree

up ahead, stopping once I was behind it.

I hope the other three managed to get out. Closing my eyes, I tried to catch my breath and prepare myself for the final leg of my journey.

"I've got you!" The voice came out of nowhere. My eyes flew open in time to see my pursuer swing.

I ducked, barely dodging his axe, the sharp blade lodging in the thick trunk behind me where my head was but mere seconds before. I screamed and ran.

"You can't run from this, Desdemona! This is fate! I will always find you!" His voice carried over the roaring winds, and I shivered, knowing it had nothing to do with the weather.

Was he right? Was this how it would

always be? Tears streamed down my face and I let myself believe that they were nothing more than the rain. I was too strong to cry. I had to be.

The ground rumbled as his large feet thundered not far behind me. In my panic, my bare feet slipped in the mud, making me stumble.

No, don't fall! I have to move!

I pushed myself up and kept going. I was so close. Two more steps, then one...

I crashed into the heavy wooden door of the barn, my hands splintering the wood enough to pierce my skin, leaving blood on the rough grain.

Why do I always leave blood behind me?

I raced in and shut the door, grabbing

a rake to bar it with.

The man laughed. "This is oddly fitting, don't you think? You dying like a trapped rat in a barn?"

WHACK.

His axe hit the door.

"I'm going to enjoy cutting you into shreds."

WHACK.

"Then I will find your friends..."

WHACK.

"...and finish them off."

WHACK.

I could see the silver glint of the axe blade as it tore through the door.

"That little girl...the redhead? She didn't look like she was doing too good... I hope she doesn't die before I can get to her."

I backed away from the door, my feet stirring up the dust and churning it into clumps of mud beneath me. Thunder crashed and the four horses screamed, rearing up and pounding on their stall doors.

I looked to each of them and saw Despair.

Finding strength in her eyes, I stood a little straighter, my eyes narrowed.

You know what you have to do. Only one of you can make it out of this barn alive.

I dropped to the ground and began to dig in the clumpy dirt with my bare hands. My nails broke, peeling back, and fingers bled, but I still kept going, not stopping until my fingers scraped cool metal.

There you are.

Wrapping my hands around the shaft, I ripped it from the earth and held it aloft.

The scythe crackled with black energy as lightning struck outside, splitting the large tree that I had used as cover in two.

The door fell.

"You're too late," I said, brandishing the weapon I was always meant to wield.

"I will kill you!" He screamed as he raced toward me, axe ready to strike. My eyes burning with the dark power inside me, I struck first, and his war cry died on his useless tongue.

"Foolish... You cannot kill Death." His blood seeped into the mud and flowed around my feet. I walked to the stall that held the first horse, a strong black mare, and released the latch.

"Come, Despair, it's time to ride," I said with one last look at the poor soul who thought he could spare the world its inevitable fate.

Why do I always have to leave blood behind me?

FAST FOOD

By Chris Bannor

The theatre was quiet when Anderson took his seat. He liked the solitude of the back row, tucked into a corner where only the occasional eye wandered before flittering away to find an available spot.

The seats had once been decorated with plush cushions in a decadent red, but age and use had rendered them a muted cousin to their original luxury. The carpets had led the path to a night of wonder and entertainment but were now nothing more than worn walkways for the bored.

He liked this movie theatre though. The staff always smiled and gave a couple of minutes of their time to him whenever he came. They had a kiosk out front to sell tickets and they kept it festive. They decorated it for the holidays with cheap props and dollar store trinkets. They had a glow in the dark Easter egg hunt for older children, handed out candy to trick or treaters at Halloween, and set up a mailbox out front for children to deliver their letters to Santa.

In a city where every other theatre was bought out and upgraded with deluxe seating and online accessibility, Anderson liked the simple charm of the run-down theatre and its second run movies.

He wasn't alone. Most nights when he came to sit through a late showing, there were plenty of guests who shared the magic of the silver screen. They trailed in— sometimes families, sometimes couples, and the occasional loner like himself.

Tonight, the tale on the screen was a tragedy, not so much in its intent but its incompetence. Anderson would wish the time back, but these days he had nothing but time on his hands. What were a few more hours wasted in front of the screen?

As the credits began to roll, the theatre emptied, and the cleaning crew began to vacuum up the spilled popcorn and discard leftover trash. Anderson meticulously threw his away and followed the rest of the movie-goers out of the building.

The parking lot was dark and eerie and in another corner of town, the residence would worry. No one thought anything of it on this side of the tracks. He watched as friends left the theatre together and went their different ways, people getting into their cars and driving away. He watched a young man at the back of the lot talking on his phone, elbows on the roof of the car with his eyes pointed down to the ground. He didn't want to intrude on the conversation, but as he stepped closer, he heard the man's voice.

"Look, I know you've been busy, but you could have at least texted me to let me know you couldn't make it tonight. I sat through the worst ninety-seven minutes of movie history by myself."

The young man hung up the phone and put it in his back pocket before he turned and saw Anderson standing two feet away. The young man registered the now-empty lot and the way they were obstructed from other eyes by trees and overgrown bushes. His brow furrowed and his hands clenched into fists, but he wasn't fast enough. He didn't even see the attack coming before Anderson pinned him to the door of his car, his face turned to the side by strong hands and an iron grip.

This was nothing like the movies. There was no hypnotic gaze to lull his victims into a tranquil state or to seduce their senses into believing this was a euphoric experience. It was shock and terror and the man beneath him struggled, even as Anderson sank his teeth into the flesh of his neck.

The young man was fighting for his life, but his struggles only gave up his life's blood quicker, each mouthful swallowed before Anderson could taste it. In the old days, he could take his time and savour each delicious pull on his victim's veins. Like everything else in the modern world, this too had lost its grandeur. Anderson was sated from the blood, but not at all satisfied with the experience.

LOCKDOWN HORROR #2

He held the man against his car and drained him until he was unconscious. The car keys were in the man's front pocket, and he threw the corpse into the passenger side before he crawled in and drove them away. When Anderson reached a random street, he pulled over and finished his meal before he left the man in his car and walked back toward the busier side of town.

Anderson stretched his arms above his head and thought about trying to find something more fulfilling, but that was a long con that he needed to plan more creatively. He smiled in anticipation though. Until then, at least he had the movies and fast food.

INTERPRETATION

By Andra Dill

Confident that his under-the-table bribe would ensure his happy future, the handsome man kissed his wan-faced wife. The proprietary kiss smeared her poppy-red lipstick.

"Show us the cards, gypsy," he demanded.

Rose accepted the shuffled Tarot cards from Aubrey's trembling hands, then dealt out three cards.

The Sun. Three of Swords. Death.

A menacing scowl darkened his face. Tears slid down Aubrey's.

"What is this?" His skin flushed fire-engine red, then morphed to dusky blue. He clutched his throat and gasped for air.

A bleak-eyed Aubrey slipped off her wedding ring.

Rose accepted her payment, then said, "Keep the lipstick."

OPEN WINDOWS

By Frederick Pangbourne

My name is George Hart, and I am a true native New Yorker. Born and raised in the great empire state. My mother, Maria, gave birth to me right here in the Bronx, over at the Lincoln Medical Centre. I was told it was during a record cold spell on a frigid February morning back in '38. I grew up in the south Bronx in one of those old, five storied apartment buildings right off Lafayette Avenue. One of those decrepit looking, brick faced apartment buildings that are practically erected right on top of each other. Like the ones on television, where the guys are running from building to building on their rooftops and leaping onto the next roof in a single bound. I always hated having all those buildings built so close to each other. So close that the residences could run a clothesline from their windows to the building next door. Cramming as much living space as possible into that one block. Yet, here I am again.

LOCKDOWN HORROR #2

My mother recently passed away two months after my forty-third birthday. I got the call at work. I was working at a buddy's garage up in Yonkers at the time. The police told me it looked as if she had a heart attack. Died in her sleep. Never knew mom as having a bad ticker but shit happens as they say. After the funeral, I decided to head back to the Bronx from Yonkers and move into our old apartment. The rent was a lot cheaper and Raymond, who's garage I was working at, had made a phone call and got me a job at a garage that was only a few blocks away from the old place near Randall avenue. The lord taketh away and he giveth.

The apartment was on the third floor of the five and faced the street out front. I left most of the things in the apartment the way they were when I moved back in. Even left mom's room the way it was. I felt bad just at the thought of getting rid of any of her stuff, so I let the room be. I wound up settling into my old bedroom. The bed seemed to have shrunk considerably since I was in it last. My feet hanging just over the edge of the mattress. Once I saved up a few bucks, I'd have to look in to replacing the bed. I made a mental note to myself of making that one of my first priorities.

It took me until the beginning of May before I was finally feeling settled in at both the old apartment and the new job. I even made the acquaintance of a couple of my neighbours in the building. There was an old black couple up on the fifth floor—

Horace and Sophia Coogan. They were somewhere in their late sixties. Real nice people. They had been living here for the longest time. When I mentioned to them that I was Maria's son, they said they remembered me as a small boy, even though I had no recollection of them. Either way, good people. Then there was a Puerto Rican girl on the floor below me—Lucinda Estevez. I never asked her how old she was, as that is just something you never ask a woman, so I'd have to guesstimate that she was somewhere in her late thirties. Beautiful woman with olive-coloured skin and long black hair and big dark eyes. I had run into her several times prior as we were getting mail from our mailboxes downstairs before I finally got up the nerve to start up a conversation. She lived alone and had moved in just over a year before me.

As May was sliding by and summer was getting ready to make its scorching grand entrance into the ghettos of the Bronx, Horace had asked me one day if I wouldn't mind looking at their car. He could only describe the problem with their old blue Pinto as 'not running right'. I felt obligated as a neighbour, and a mechanic, to take a gander beneath the hood and see what was cooking. It was during that overcast Saturday afternoon when I went out to the street with my toolbox that I first became aware of the night crawler. Ole' Horace must have felt a little guilty having me out there at the curb looking under the hood by myself, or maybe Sophia had coaxed him out there to keep me company as I gave the engine a going over. He stood leaning against the car with his hands crammed in his pockets, gazing up at the neighbouring apartments that lined our street.

"Gonna be a hot summer," he stated to no one in particular, his eyes scanning the facades of the surrounding buildings. "The night crawler is gonna have a grand old time this year."

"The who?" I asked from under hood as I was checking the spark plug tips.

"The night crawler," he repeated nonchalantly. "Your mamma never told you about her?"

"I can't say she ever did. Who is she?

Some homeless lady?"

Horace chuckled at my inquiry. "No. I wish that's all she was. She comes out every summer, hoping to find some poor soul with their windows wide open on a hot summer night."

His statement had drawn my curiosity, and I emerged from under the hood, still running a folded piece of sandpaper between a plug's electrode and arm. "What?"

Horace turned his eyes from the urban landscape and faced me. "Some folks think it's just some silly urban legend, but I've seen her with my own two eyes, so I know better. You'll find none of my windows open at night during the summer, no sir, and I'd advise you to do the same."

I was the one chuckling now. "What are you talking about?"

He leaned closer and lowered his tone slightly as a woman and her three kids passed us on the sidewalk. "They say that there's an old Haitian woman who lives somewhere here in the Bronx. Exactly where, I don't know, nor do I want to. Came over on the boat a long time ago. They say she's a Mambo."

"Mambo?" I now found myself leaning on the car next to him. The engine was a distant memory.

"A voodoo priestess. They say she's older than you, me and Sophia all put together. She's still alive after all this time because of that night crawler. She sends it out on summer nights to suck the life outta people while they sleep, then it crawls back to her before the sun rises and breaths the life of those folks into her. That's what keeps her alive for so long."

I found the yarn that Horace was spinning as entertaining as it was captivating and went along with his fabricated story. "So exactly what is this…night crawler?"

"Well, to be honest, the night crawler is what I call it. Its true name is 'Le Rodeur'."

"Le… Ro.." I struggled to repeat the foreign word.

"Le Rodeur. It's a French word. Means something that creeps or prowls around, or something of the sort. Shit, I'm not French, that's why I call it the night crawler.

Anyway, this thing looks something like a big black spider, but it's not really a spider exactly. It has part of a woman mixed in there. Something that priestess called up from some hole in hell."

"A spider? Mixed with a woman?" *Horace's imagination is without limits.*

"Only way I can describe it. I didn't believe in all that bullshit voodoo mumbo jumbo either, until I saw it myself. Was about five or six summers ago. I woke up in the middle of the night to take a piss. When you get old, you find yourself always having to piss. Anyway, as most folks here do in the summer who can't afford an air conditioner or the electric bill that comes with it, they leave their windows wide open all night, hoping that some kind of breeze blows in during the night to offer a little relief from the heat while they're sleeping."

I nodded as I listened. I recalled how my mother had always kept all the windows wide open at night during the summer. Even with one of those small, oscillating fans going on all night, I remembered just lying there in the dark, spread eagle on the sheets in nothing but my skivvies, trying to cool off from the stifling heat.

"Well, I was standing there in front of the john, pissing and looking out the small window above it. At first, I thought I was seeing things but, after rubbing the sleep from my eyes, I found out I wasn't. I saw this giant spider crawling on the building across the way. It blended in with the night's shadows and was as silent as the grave as it moved. I watched it scurry about along the side of the wall, checking each window it came upon. When it stopped at an open one, it crawled right into that apartment. Not sure how long I stood there at the john, watching out the window, but it was sometime long after I had finished pissing when it came back out and crawled off to the back of the building. Later the next day, come to find out that Mr. Jackson was found dead in that apartment."

I realised just how distracting his story had become and moved back to the engine. I didn't want to spend all afternoon under the hood. "That was probably just a coincidence. Like you said, it was dark, there were shadows, and you had just awakened. A perfect combination to be seeing hallucinations."

"Hallucinations, my dick! I know what I saw. This thing, like some spider woman, crawls about the sides of buildings at night looking for an open window so it can creep in and suck the life outta someone in their sleep. If you're smart, you'll take my—"

"Horace!" Sophia was calling down from their window five floors up. "Come on up for lunch. Got soup and a sandwich waiting on you!"

"Just keep your widows closed at night, George. At least until summer passes." With his parting words, Horace pulled himself from off the car and patted my shoulder as he shuffled into the building.

LOCKDOWN HORROR #2

As I was checking and cleaning the other spark plugs, I found myself still smiling at his urban legend and how seriously he took it. I thought about how hot their apartment must get in the summer at night, with only a small fan going and all the windows sealed because of one old superstitious man. I laughed out loud and shook my head as I continued with my task.

****

Just like Horace had predicted that Saturday afternoon, summer had come early and with a blazing introduction. The sweltering humidity seemed to linger all day long, making the simple act of breathing a laborious effort, and still it mocked and defied you as it remained even in the dark of night. During the past couple of weeks, I had become closer with Lucinda, and we saw more of one another other outside of just bumping into each other at the mailbox. On a couple of occasions, we even went out to a local pub down the street for a couple of beers. In that time, we had become comfortable enough with each other to exchange apartment keys. Not that there was anything serious going on between us but, we just trusted one another enough to hold on to the other's key just in case we got locked out. It was easier this way instead of waking the building's super up late at night just to tell him you were locked out.

It had been just over a month after we

had exchanged keys when it happened. I had come home late one Friday night from the garage and the heat that day just seemed to drain the strength from me. Ya know the feeling? All I wanted to do when I walked in that door was flop on the couch and knock back a few cold beers and watch some television. I eventually wound up calling Lucinda to see if she wanted to hang out and share a few drinks. Maybe even go down to the pub where there was air conditioning, but there was no answer at her place. Probably out on a date or with some friends. I decided to make the best of the evening and settled for some cold Coors and back-to-back episodes of The Honeymooners.

I couldn't tell you what time I had

fallen asleep. One minute I was five beers in, watching Ralph and Norton preparing to buy a hotdog stand, and the next, I was sound asleep. Something, though, had awakened me from my clammy slumber sometime past midnight. I slowly opened my eyes and saw there was nothing on the television now but static. The network was done for the night, and the apartment was dark. As I laid there on the couch with my clothes sticking to me with sweat, I debated if I should jump in the shower and try to cool off before I went to my bed for the rest of the night. Before I could come to any conclusion on the matter, the noise that had initially awakened me came again. A creaking of a floorboard. It came from the kitchen behind the couch.

LOCKDOWN HORROR #2

I had grown up in this apartment and knew it as well as one might an old, close friend. I knew which windows leaked cold drafts in the winter, which wall sockets worked, and which didn't and especially what areas of the hardwood floor creaked when stepped upon. I gently closed my eyes and feigned sleep as I awaited my next move. The floor creaked again ever so slightly as pressure was placed on its surface. Someone had somehow managed to get into my apartment. I racked my brain for anything close at hand that I could use as a weapon. I strained on picturing a mental image of my surrounding area on the couch and could find nothing that would aid me in a fight. Empty beer cans and a tv remote would not cut the mustard.

I thought, if I were to perhaps suddenly flying off the couch, screaming like some madman, that it would give me the element of surprise and maybe even the upper hand, but that notion was swept aside when I felt a weight being applied to the couch itself. Was somebody climbing onto the couch with me? I slowly allowed my eyelids to part as I could no longer cluelessly lie there, oblivious to what was taking place. I damn near screamed and pissed myself.

Though my eyes were beholding what was squatting over me, my mind was mentally screaming that this could not be reality, but a horrifying nightmare that I could not awaken from. The ghastly monstrosity was directly over me, balanced partially on both the couch and the floor. I instantly recognised it as some giant, man-sized spider. Four of its long, segmented legs were perched on the back of the couch while the other four rested on the floor between the tv and I. The foul creature was huge and black with splashes of grey mixed into its body, giving it superb camouflage for its night-time patrols amongst the shadows. The most hideous aspect of this abomination was its head. Horace was indeed correct about it being a female. A human head was fixed where the spider's face should have been. A haggard looking grey face of a woman with long, matted black hair that dangled about my face. The eyes in the ungodly face were a milky white. All four of them! Two more smaller eyes bulged from the forehead. The misshapen mouth was even more grotesque. Two small infant-like arms stretched from the sides of its head and constantly moved about, its tiny pointed fingers grasping at the air and its little hands playfully touching the creature's dripping maw.

As I had said, I did not scream, I couldn't, but I sure as hell pissed myself though. I was literally paralyzed with fear as I lay there in sweat and urine. The face loomed closer and the spider's sternum lowered itself onto me and I could now feel its weight. The tiny hands reached out and began to gently stroke my face as it was lining its mouth directly onto mine. I was about to have the life sucked from me and they would find me sprawled out dead on the couch in the morning, like Mr Jackson.

"George?" Someone was calling my name outside my door and began knocking louder than one should. "George, you up? I forgot my key."

My god! Not her. Please don't let it take her. I mentally cried as the sudden noise startled it, causing it to lift itself off me. The head turned toward the door as Lucinda called my name again and knocked. "I'm gonna come in and get my key, okay? I hope you're decent." I could hear her fumbling my spare key into the door's lock.

The face turned back to meet mine and the little hands again caressed my face. "Soon." It spoke in a gurgled hiss, and in one quick movement, it was off both me and the couch. As the front door swung open, I heard it brush against the kitchen window on its way out, rattling the glass pane as it passed through.

Even as Lucinda walked in and saw me lying on the couch, surrounded by beer cans and in my piss stained pants, I still couldn't move. What I had just experienced was so surreal that my mind was still trying to sort through what had just happened when she looked down at me in disgust.

"Jesus Christ, George. What the fuck? Look at yourself." Was all she said as she walked over to the wall and pulled her key off the nail it hung from. She looked down at me again, shook her head in disappointment, and scoffed before she walked out. Still, I just lay there in a hot mess and in silence. I could only imagine the sight I must have been.

It took a good five minutes to process everything that had occurred and chalk it up to something that was dreadfully real and not some baneful dream. When I finally accepted the ordeal, I recalled the one word that thing spoke before it scurried back out the window. Soon. It was then I leapt from the couch and began closing and securing all the windows to the apartment, as well as closing all the shades. As the reality of my experience soaked in, my legs and hands began to shake. I reached into the cabinet above the sink and pulled out a bottle of the hard stuff. I must confess that I had never been so scared in all my life and I turned on every light then sat at that kitchen table all night pulling off that bottle until the sun rose. Only then did I move to my bedroom and succumb to a restless sleep.

I awoke the next morning with the notion that last night's events were in no way accurate and just a far-off dream. The idea was almost accepted until I sat up, still in yesterday's clothes, and saw the front of my pants were still damp with piss. With it being daylight and the temperature already rising, I pulled myself from my bed and showered. The whole time I stood under the cool cascade of water, I tried to tell myself that it couldn't have been real. After changing into some fresh clothes, I finished what was left in the bottle and went up to see Horace.

LOCKDOWN HORROR #2

To my luck, Sophia had run out to do some food shopping, leaving Horace and myself alone for the time being. Before I could unload my experience onto him, he poured us each a shot of blackberry brandy. He said that, by the look on my face, I needed it. It was after the third shot that I told him of last night's encounter. There were times where I stammered through my story and at one point almost cried but, with much difficulty and two more shots of brandy, I finally concluded my tale.

"Sounds to me like that young girl saved your ass last night," he finally said. "It also sounds like the night crawler isn't through with you yet."

"What do you mean?"

"If that thing told you 'soon' what'cha

think that means, huh? Sounds to me like she's gonna be paying you another visit."

"But why?" I was already starting to sweat despite the old box fan that was mounted in the window and failing to blow any cool air into the room.

"You denied it a life, and you got a pretty good look at it, I guess. Only thing I can tell you, George, is that you are one lucky mutha fucker; and you owe that girl downstairs even though she has no idea what she did."

"Yeah, I guess I do." I stood up and set the shot glass on an end table near my chair. "I've got to get going, Horace. I'm still having a hard time swallowing all this. I need to do some thinking."

"You do all the thinking you need to

and most of all, make sure your windows are locked up every night now." He stood, too, and walked me to the door.

Every summer night since then, I closed and secured all those windows religiously. I didn't give a damn how hot it got in that tiny apartment those windows stayed shut. It took me the rest of that summer before I stopped closing my blinds at night. Eventually my life began to slowly resume its normal day-to-day activities, and I even started talking to Lucinda again. You see, after that night she avoided me and had even given me back the key to my place. She must have thought I was some drunken vagrant after what she saw that night. I never mentioned what really happened and never will. After that day up in Horace's apartment, I never spoke a word of it again and Horace never brought up the subject.

Sometimes, over the last few summers, while I lay there in bed on those sweltering nights, spread eagle in my skivvies, just as I had done as a child, I would catch a glimpse of some dark shadow move quietly passed one of my windows. I didn't try to summon up some reasonable explanation to the shape or begin to deny what was really out there crawling around, because I knew exactly what it was. Le Rodeur. The night crawler. During its late-night prowling about the city, it was occasionally making a detour just to see if I had let down my guard and accidently left a window open.

LOCKDOWN HORROR #2

Last summer, Horace passed away. No, not by the night crawler. He still kept his windows closed every summer like clockwork. He had tripped carrying a bag of groceries up the steep stairs to his apartment. The poor bastard broke his neck in the fall. Killed him instantly, some say. I was at work when it occurred and found out from Lucinda later that day as we met at our mailboxes. A month later, Sophia moved away and was staying with family down in North Carolina. As for Lucinda, we gradually started hanging out once more and even exchanged keys again. The lord taketh away and he giveth.

Things were finally starting to fall back into a comfortable state of normality. I even spent some money I had stashed away for a new couch and bought an air conditioner for Lucinda. I never forgot what Horace had said about me owing that girl for her unexpected arrival that night and saving my ass from a horrible death. The least I could do was give her a reason to close her windows in the summer. I think my gift won me major brownie points because we are going out next weekend for dinner. This relationship may just be ready to progress to the next level.

I was coming home from that pub down the street where Lucinda and I used to frequent, only this time I was out celebrating one of my co-worker's birthdays. All the guys from the garage were there. Despite the day's earlier heat, there was a slight breeze in the air that night, and it felt good as I walked home. The pleasantry was short lived though as I entered my building and climbed the stairs to the third floor. I was sweating like a bull by the time I reached my door.

As soon I walked in and closed the door behind me, I could tell she had been in my apartment. Her perfume still lingered in the air as I walked into the darkened confines inside. The only light on was the overhead light above the stove. A folded piece of paper was neatly placed on the stove's surface. My name was written across it. I was already smiling as I unfolded the paper and read the hand-written note:

George,

I just wanted to tell you how much I

appreciate the air conditioner and how much I appreciate you. We've really come a long way since you first moved in. To show you how much I appreciate your efforts, I bought a bottle of wine and will probably have started it by the time you read this. How about coming downstairs and helping me finish it?

Lucinda

P.S. Opened a few of the windows to let some air in. There's a beautiful breeze out tonight. How you can have them closed all summer is beyond me.

My smile faded as quickly as it had formed, and the letter slipped from fingers. I could only stare straight ahead as I heard something shifting in the room's darkness.

LOCKDOWN HORROR #2

It pushed aside a chair behind me as it was moving closer. A black shadow began to fall over me. I closed my eyes as tightly as possible. "Finally," the gurgled hiss spat into my ear. This time I did scream.

THE WEATHERMASTER

**By Christopher T. Dabrowski,
translated by Julia Mraczny**

Whenever my knee hurt, it would rain. I'm a meteopath. Which also involves sleepiness and headaches.

One night I had an amazing dream. I dreamt that I had a little switch in my knee, which changes the weather. When it hurts me there, it switches to rain.

Awake, I touched my knee and felt something. I pressed once, twice, and nothing. I hit it with my fist. Nothing.

Like something old, it's resistant.

I went to get a hammer. I hit it. It hurt, but the tearing went away. Storm clouds were also breaking up. It was another sunny day.

FLOCK

By David Green

From the safety of the barn roof, Peterson held his shotgun with a loose grip, mouth agape as he stared below us. The moon shone above, full and beautiful.

Moans returned my attention to the

ground. Thousands of them in every direction, moving as one towards us.

"They're like a flock of sheep," Peterson said, shaking his head.

I peered over the roof's edge. The crowd pressed themselves against the barn; the ones in front falling and those behind climbing on them.

"That shotgun loaded?" I asked, taking a step backwards.

"Two shells left."

We both knew what that meant.

THE WATCHER

By Jacqueline Moran Meyer

My boots crush the virgin snow as I labour through the storm. I jostle past a patch of close-knit trees. Hidden branches catch my gloved hands, which are splayed in front of my face, protecting my eyes from injury. The noise coming from the snapping twigs worries me, as does the risk of falling into a white camouflaged ditch. No moon or stars guide my path, as the snowfall obscures all light, but carrying a flashlight will draw unwanted attention. Trespassing through rural properties requires stealth.

A comforting scent of burning wood fills the air. The house stands nearby. A dim yellow glow filters through the pine trees and reflects off the snow in the clearing up ahead. The light gets brighter with each step. Rescued out of near blindness, I soon find myself staring at the back of Melody's home.

The old pink Victorian house appears

immaculate and small. The windows cast the natural brilliance of a household at night. Smoke billows from the chimney, and I imagine the warmth friends would find inside, but I remain unwelcome.

The structure resembles a sturdy dollhouse. Miniature modern furniture, tiny lamps, and petite original art decorate the interior of the house. All this pure splendour exists for the living dolls moving about on the shiny wood floors. A life I watch others live without me.

Melody is washing dishes in her kitchen sink. Her beauty faded this year. A pale, puffy face with dead eyes stares out the window as I stare inside. Dirty, drab hair with dark roots replaces her once long blonde straight hair. Wrinkles crease her brow, and deep smoker's lines stream down the corners of her mouth. No longer slim, her jawline is gone and replaced with a fold of fat.

A light brightens an upstairs room, and I glance up and to the top right window. The oldest daughter sits on a bed staring at something in her lap, perhaps a phone or a book. Oh, great. The girl wears headphones and won't be able to hear me come in.

Peering back into the downstairs kitchen window, I don't see Melody. Hoping my black ski outfit will cloak me in invisibility, I step sideways, and hunker down behind a nearby bush. The view of the inside of the house improves from here. The young twin girls sit on the floor of the family room in front of the fireplace, playing a board game. Their mother speaks to them with her lined mouth and flails her arms as she explains something, like a puppet manipulated by strings from someone up above.

The twins race through the hallway to the front door. Melody turns on the foyer light and opens the thick oak door. The husband, Matt, smiles as he enters the home. The couple kisses before Matt bends down and picks up the girls with his broad frame and muscular arms. The five-year-old girls wipe the snow off his handsome head.

The happy family sits down at the table to eat while the older daughter remains in her room.

The four of them stopped eating at the

exact same time and set down their forks. For a second, I think they notice me outside, but as they look up at the ceiling, I realise who must be making noise. Matt smiles and makes a hand gesture to his family, which suggests they should continue eating. The daddy of four girls walks up the back staircase from the kitchen that leads to the baby's room. A moment later, the nursery light goes on. Matt picks up the prize. There she is, pretty in pink. He kisses their darling, chubby four-month-old giggling girl several times on her cheeks and neck. His smile, an expression of pure joy.

Matt exits the nursery. In a few minutes, I see him enter the oldest child's room, beautiful baby in hand. They startle the preteen who rips off her headphones to yell at her dad, then puts them back on. He shrugs his shoulders and kisses her petulant head before leaving the room—spoiled kids.

I am watching them all play with the baby. She is the complete focus of their attention.

I met Melody a year ago through Sara, a mutual friend. Sara divorced and decided to move to London. The three of us ate a pleasant meal together before her move. Sara and I became friends in college, but we didn't see each other often over the years because she moved quite a lot. Like me, she had no children. Melody and Sara met through work. Advertising, I surmised.

Unemployed, unmarried, and

childless, I moved back in with my parents at the age of forty-two. Meeting Melody felt like a gift. Three months pregnant at the time, she glowed with health and happiness. Although she didn't work, I pretended to be impressed with her food pantry drives, girl scout troop, and PTA presidency. By the end of the evening, we exchanged telephone numbers.

When we first became friends, we spoke on the phone, and I visited her, about four weeks later, at her house. Five months into the relationship I remained unemployed and hated living with my judgemental parents.

Melody had four weeks until her due date.

By month seven, still unemployed, I

called twice a day. I liked calling Melody. Her voice comforted me; I felt less lonely. I also pretended to enjoy listening to her speak about her pregnancy. By this point, I believed she thought of me as her best friend. Her sister visited all the time.

The sister's jealousy came between us. Made evident by the fact, I never received an invitation to her house again.

"Hello, Andrea. No luck finding a job? I'm sorry...." Sara said, answering my phone call. The fourth of the day. She sounded cold.

In the background, I heard her sister speak in a hushed but loud tone. I think she wanted me to be able to make out what she said.

"Is it her again? You are way too

accommodating. Hang up! She is scary crazy. I know you pity her, but she isn't your responsibility. Mama always said, 'Melody always tries to save the strays.' Sometimes strays scratch. Stop it!"

Melody kept on speaking, unaware I heard everything her sister said. What a bitch!

She enacted 'Martial Law' and placed extreme communication limits on me.

"Hello, Andrea. I'm due any day now and almost ready to burst. It's hectic getting the kids up, cooking breakfast, and making sure we can arrive at school on time. I can't talk on the phone. I'm sure you understand."

One day, I heard from Melody. A healthy baby arrived! I wanted to visit.

LOCKDOWN HORROR #2

"Hi, Andrea. I know you didn't mean to, but the phone woke my baby girl. It took me a long time to put her down to sleep. Don't call around nap time. Sorry!"

"Sorry, I am not up for visitors."

"Can't talk. The kids are walking off the bus."

Eight months into the friendship, she started responding a lot less and sending back shorter and colder texts.

Dinner time. I am feeling a little blue today. Might be postpartum crap. I am not sure.

Bath time. I wish I could grow eight hands when needed.

Matt's home.

The whole family is here.

Super busy.

Sick.

Hectic.

I'm overwhelmed.

I blamed her sister. Our relationship changed after I overheard what the jealous psycho said as I spoke to Melody on the phone. She ruined everything by shining a light of mistrust on me. Melody stopped texting back. I couldn't leave phone messages at all because her voice mail was full. I guess she never listened to any of them.

Soon, she stopped interacting with me. She ghosted me! I realised she never called me. Ever. Not once. She now used the new baby as an excuse.

I will not come last!

With great difficulty, I didn't call

Melody for thirty days. I worried about her and the baby. I disguised myself and took trips, using my parent's boring car to pass by her house, trying to catch a glimpse of them.

I called after the four weeks passed, and she answered.

"Hi. My sister passed away nineteen days ago. She died in an accident. It's not easy for me to cope, let alone care for the baby. I stopped nursing her. The police believe she hit a patch of black ice as she drove to work early in the morning. She skidded off the road, and the car flipped, crashing down a steep embankment. When she didn't show up for surgery, the hospital called, and we called everyone we knew. The police found her dead."

Melody sobbed for an hour, and I listened; in heaven, she needed me.

What Melody didn't know was, I followed her sister for a week to memorise her schedule. She drove to work before dawn on Wednesdays. There is one short, curvy stretch on Elk Mountain without a protective guardrail against the steep drop. With luck, if I hit her bumper at the right time, her car would fly off of the road. There would be no paint or residue from my vehicle. I brought my unlicensed gun I bought from some thug in Florida with me. I would use it if necessary.

I followed the bitch from her house. I sped up as I drove up the mountain. I crept close behind her, honking my horn, trying to scare and distract her. I got to the spot where no median protected her from the sheer drop off the mountain. I rammed into the back of her car, travelling 30 miles an hour. She swerved and lost control of her vehicle. As I watched her car fall over the ledge of the 100-foot drop, I crossed my fingers and prayed she would die.

I started calling Melody every day again, and sometimes, she answered, and I listened to her cry. I thought an invitation would be imminent. Maybe after she got over her sister's death, but none came.

She stopped picking up my telephone calls, and she didn't answer any of my hundreds of text messages. Enough! Ten days ago, I showed up at her front door with a cake and flowers. No one answered, although I saw movement in the house and her car in the driveway. Rude! Mean! It took me hours in bumper to bumper traffic to drive there. I fumed as I drove back to my house. I threw the flowers out the window on the highway and ate the cake with my bare hands, shoving fistfuls of it into my mouth. Too busy? Or too busy for me?

Oh, please! The woman didn't work and spent her time preparing peanut butter sandwiches. Why would anyone prefer to help other people's dreams come true instead of their own? I don't understand. She must be so bored. I may be unemployed at the moment, but I have a career. She's a babysitter, a laundress, and his plaything.

Melody doesn't know how many ways

I could destroy her character. People want to believe lies. A spoken lie always becomes someone's truth. I could say she is cheating, abusive, intoxicated, or suicidal. But I won't, because I want something else from her.

When I went back home, I called eighteen times before Matt picked up.

"Listen closely, Andrea. I am only going to say this once. We obtained a restraining order against you. My wife pitied you, but you cannot take unsubtle hints, can you? Do *not* come to my home again. Leave us alone. You're not welcome. Am I clear?"

Pitied me?

After he hung up and blocked me, I went into plan B mode and began orchestrating the plans for tonight.

My problems are worse!

I gave up looking for work. My past employers would not give me a decent reference. Thank goodness for the money I won from the harassment lawsuit from my old place of employment. My boss would not go the next step to cement our relationship. How dare he humiliate me! I recorded him, saying he found me to be attractive. I edited out the parts where he said he had no feelings for me, and he would report me for my stalking behaviour against him. He pressed me to ask for help and called me delusional!

Angry at the rejection and false accusations, I acted first. I told the managing partners he harassed me for ages with unwanted attention, holding on to my doctored recording as proof. I destroyed the bastard's life. They fired him, and his wife took the kids and filed for divorce. The police discovered his body in the garage with the car running later in the week. He committed suicide. What a baby!

The company found an accounting discrepancy I made and used the mistake as an excuse to fire me soon after his death.

Now, here I am, standing in a snowstorm.

I continue to observe the family wind down for the evening until the house becomes dark.

Patience.

I wait.

Thank goodness, they don't own an

alarm. Melody doesn't know I stole a house key. I took it from their key rack in the kitchen months ago—long before they banned me. The bastards!

The snow will cover my tracks after walking back to the car I parked several blocks away.

I can take one. Melody will still be a mother to three.

I will lurk up the back staircase. The baby's room is conveniently down the hall from the other bedrooms. I brought my gun in case anyone wakes up.

The infant will not remember them, and I'll try out being a mom.

My parents will be glad to be rid of me. I am tired of hearing how I exhaust them and abuse them. My psychiatric hospital

LOCKDOWN HORROR #2

stints drained them of their retirement funds. I don't want to pay for their rent in *their* old age. I placed the fake suicide note on my mom's pillow. They won't search long for me.

A suitcase filled with the lawsuit cash sits in my trunk.

I bought a car seat and baby supplies n my ride up to Melody's house.

My new daughter and I will drive until we disappear.

No one will find us, and Melody will suffer, as she should.

Previously published in Yellow Mama 'eZine, 2019

LOCKDOWN HORROR #2

AN UNKNOWN FACT

By Galina Trefil

Stealing the boat was a sound plan, the

friends thought. Sustained by the ocean's fish, they'd drift away from their town's blood-curling chaos until the danger had passed.

Over time, their binoculars showed them that, as the living's screams from the mainland began to quiet, the numbers of the risen dead grew ever-larger, making the boat's return impossible.

For the boat dwellers, lethargy set in, gums bled, skin yellowed, and insides haemorrhaged.

For months, they'd survived falling prey to monsters. To repel their scurvy, they only needed to eat the kelp floating near the shore... A fact they never realised.

SOMETHING WICKED LIVES IN THE WOODS

By E.L. Giles

There were four to begin with. Four long-time friends crowded in a decrepit truck and headed north for a hunting trip in Ruby Lake Provincial Park. Their rifles were packed in the cargo bed, and their camping equipment, ammo, fuel, and provisions were secured. They had all the necessities for their one-week trip into the Canadian wilderness. Nothing could dull their excitement or tarnish this moment for them—the trip had been a year in the making. From the search for their camping spot to their daily itinerary, they'd thought of everything and they were ready to face anything.

Black spruce, pine, and white cedars stood sentinel as the friends drove past, while the overgrown maples and birch, stripped of their colourful robes, exposed their skeletal limbs for the wind to buffet.

Here, nature lay untouched, and the rows of tightly clustered trees formed an impassable wall, fathomless and surreal to anyone, save those who knew where to look and what to look for.

"Did you spot some?" asked Johnny, the youngest of the group. He craned his neck towards the window opposite to his seat, where Jake sat. Staring intently, Johnny continued, "Any moose or deer? Are we too early in the season?"

Jake sighed. He shook his head and answered gravely, "Nothing past Thunder Bay."

Something concerned Jake about the surrounding desolation. But at the same time, it also intrigued him, calling to the native blood that coursed through his veins like an omen. Something in the air was reaching out for his soul, asking him to leave, it seemed. It was a feeling more than anything palpable. Jake didn't know what to think about it and how he could tell his friend about the matter of his concerns. How could he explain to them that the forest seemed to be rejecting them? How could he justify the cold that crept up his spine as he recalled the aeons-old stories of his people? Stories about *something* lurking in the woods, gaunt and starving, rabid and hungry for fresh human flesh. A beast inhabited by the spirit of the forest and intent on repelling invaders as well as games and every living thing around it.

Jake let the grim sensation pass. Those were just fairy tales, after all. How could they be otherwise?

"At least we've got enough beers," said Bobby, who was seated in front of Jake.

Shane rolled his eyes from behind the steering wheel. "That's little girl juice." He picked up the bottle of scotch clamped between his legs and gulped. He then brandished it for everyone to see. "That's a real man's drink."

"Couldn't you just drive and stop drinking?" Johnny said, snatching the bottle from Shane's hand.

"Hey! Give it back—"

Shane screamed suddenly. Instinctively, he slammed on the brakes, and some thirty yards later the pickup finally stopped.

"What the fuck is wrong with you?" yelled Bobby, who had knocked his head against the dashboard.

"Some…something crossed the road. It was…" Shane's heart galloped. He clenched the steering wheel with white knuckles, waiting for the shivers to pass. He then rubbed his eyes, as if they might have deceived him. Gathering his remaining courage, he opened the door of the truck and inhaled as much fresh air as he could. That was the only way Shane knew to help quell the nearly debilitating panic.

"What?" Jake inquired, concerned. "What was it?"

The breeze wafted in an effluvium of earth and rot, along with the characteristic smell of cedar and pine. Shane breathed deeply, becoming calmer, until the wind shifted suddenly, as if intending to disrupt his serenity. Shane sniffed, nauseated by the acrid and vile combination of decay and wet animal fur. The next moment, the stench was gone, and the wind had stopped attacking his nostrils. He got back into the truck, forgetting about the odour, and closed the door. He looked at Jake through the rear-view mirror, and they quickly exchanged a worried glance.

"A deer, most likely," Shane said. "Or a moose. Anyway, it's gone."

It ended up being an isolated incident, and they resumed their journey up to the lake, where they intended to camp. Even after they had finished erecting the tent and building a proper campfire, nothing queer happened. Though the laughter and conversation were happy and light-hearted, and the beer and scotch flowed abundantly, there reigned an unsettling silence that, to Jake, seemed totally unnatural. The hairs on his neck were raised; Jake couldn't kill the awkward sensation of being observed, of not being alone despite the silence and the stillness surrounding them. The event on the road was at the forefront of his mind, and unable to keep it to himself anymore, he decided to tackle the matter with Shane.

He waited until Johnny and Bobby were passed out drunk before handing Shane the bottle of scotch.

"A real man's drink, eh?" Jake jerked his head towards Bobby and Johnny, who had together siphoned about a quarter of the bottle and were now snoring noisily.

Shane smiled, but it didn't reach his eyes. He then shook his head, refusing the drink he normally indulged in happily. Jake sat closer to Shane and searched his eyes— searched for something within them. He was certain the terror would be playing in them like a film on a loop. And he found it, living within the many strands of green and brown colouring Shane's irises. The fire was lively, cracking softly and warmly, though neither Jake nor Shane found comfort in it.

"What did you see on the road?"

"I told you. A deer, or something like that."

"C'mon, buddy. The thing scared the

shit out of you. What was it?" Jake became more insistent, clutching Shane's forearm.

Shane stared into the fire, as if seeking courage to put into words the thing he'd seen.

"I couldn't see it that well, you know, you know. It had antlers, and it was freakishly tall," Shane said.

"More like a moose then?"

Shane turned his head and stared straight into Jake's dark eyes. He shook his head.

"No!" he said, his voice breaking. "It walked on *two* legs. Like a human. And the thing was scary thin—skeletal. And its *skin*…it was the colour of ash. And when I was outside the truck, I smelt it. I can't describe it, the odour, but all that it made me think of was death." Shane finally took the bottle of scotch from Jake's hand and sipped at it. "You think I'm crazy, huh?"

"Bobby and Johnny certainly would," Jake said, but he believed Shane. "Did it see you? I mean, did it look straight into your eyes?"

"What? No!" Shane shouted, almost insulted.

Jake frowned. "You sure?"

The creature's blazing eyes, fathomless, flashed into Shane's memory. Truly, they'd pierced through his soul and corrupted him in a way he couldn't explain. The sensation was far too crazy to admit, so Shane simply shook his head.

"Okay then." Jake remained silent for a moment, thoughtful. "It sounds like the

Man-Eater. A man who has been corrupted by the spirit of the forest and who seeks fresh human flesh. In the old legends from my people, it is called *Wendigo*."

The word died with an eerie echo, and both men avoided speaking for a few moments. They honoured the mystic silence with their own muteness. Jake, though, studied the silence. He considered it and pondered the stories his people had been telling for ages about the creature.

"I'm going to bed," Shane finally said, stepping over his passed-out friends and disappearing into the tent.

Jake didn't go to sleep though. Instead, he went to the entrance of the clearing where they'd set up camp and kneeled there, his back to the lake and the tent. He stared into the darkness ahead. Closing his eyes, he tried to empty his mind and enter into a close communion with nature, summoning the spirit of the forest the way the shaman did.

Though unaccustomed to such a practice, Jake did as best he could to remember the entire process and the prayer. He finished with, "Spare us your wrath. Spare us your hunger. Keep the beast away from us, and do not call Shane to you. Tomorrow, we will leave by the first rays of sunlight and never come back."

A sudden breeze arose, carrying with it strange and ghostly echoes and murmurs that troubled Jake deeply. The noises quickly built, coming from everywhere around him, as if the forest was slowly closing and engulfing him in its gluttonous mouth. The sensation left a layer of cold sweat on Jake's dark skin, forcing him to seek comfort near the fire, where he could keep watch until dawn.

Guided by the low moon, Jake moved stealthily back towards the campfire. He momentarily let the moonlight draw his attention as it reflected over the rippling water in the lake until something entered his line of vision—two glowing spots, radiating into the dark night behind the nearest row of black spruce. A dark, monstrously tall shape began to materialise. Before Jake could focus more intently, it had disappeared. For an unaccustomed observer, such a thing might have gone unnoticed or been ignored. But

Jake knew. The trees swayed, and twigs and branches cracked. Jake could easily follow its advance from where he was positioned in the clearing. The thing moved impossibly fast, approaching the camp with inhuman speed.

Without hesitation, Jake ran into the woods in a restless chase after the horned beast. Its vile, awful smell floated statically like a fetid cloud of death wherever it passed, leaving an easy trail for Jake to follow.

Through sharp branches and protruding ferns, rounding overgrown pines and round, moss-covered rocks, Jake ran after the beast until the evil smell, as well as the sounds of its movement, seemed to have vanished. Jake had just stopped to lean his back against a tree and breathe deeply, letting hope fill his fearful mind, when he heard a piercing, inhuman scream. It seemed to be coming from the camp.

"Shane!" Jake picked up a sharp, sturdy looking branch from the ground and ran towards the camp, as fast as his exhausted legs would carry him.

The campfire was but glowing embers now, and the moon sporadically hid behind the fluffy clouds. The darkness spread fuller and thicker during these interludes. To his left side, the tent remained intact. Could he have imagined the scream, or had he simply been tricked by the wind and the weird noises of the forest?

Then Jake realised something. Listening intently, he turned his ears towards the tent, concentrating as hard as he could. But all he heard was silence.

"Bobby? Johnny? Are you guys up?" Jake approached his friends, who had not moved an inch since passing out earlier in the evening. "Hey, guys, it's time to wake up. C'mon"

Jake tapped his branch on his friends' backs. Neither moved. He crouched and turned Bobby over. He nearly fainted at the vision of his friend, now an empty shell. Hollowed eyes and disfigured, his chest and stomach had been torn open like something had fed on him. He hastened to turn to Johnny and then fell on his rear, his entire body turning to water as he realised that his friend was in the same state as Bobby. Jake had a hard time catching his breath and fighting the retches that assailed him unstoppably. And the panic only intensified when two blazing eyes appeared through the flap of the tent.

"Shane?" Jake said, his voice barely audible. "Shane, is that you?"

The *thing* exited the tent, moving slowly and clumsily towards Jake, as if running out of energy. Jake squinted. The pale rays of the moon bathed the bloodied face and body of the *thing,* revealing the features of a man he'd once known as his friend Shane. But this thing wasn't Shane anymore. His eyes didn't reflect—not entirely—Shane's soul.

The thing whimpered as it moved and stared at the bodies of Bobby and Johnny. Jake placed himself between the bodies of his friends and *Shane* in a feeble effort to protect them, though it was entirely futile at this point.

"You did this?" said Jake, his voice renewed with strength.

Shane nodded.

"Why?"

"Hun—gry." *Shane* sat and waited. He looked to Jake like a pitiful dog, knowing he was about to be scolded. "Can't sa—tiate."

The wind rose up again, stronger, transporting echoes of voices that seemed to shake *Shane* greatly. *Shane* responded, shaking his head. His whimpers renewed, turning to heart-wrenching growls as he contorted, in prey of a sudden and excruciating pain. What humanity remained in *Shane* seemed to be fighting with the beast inside of him, the one the spirit of the forest had impregnated him with. Hearing about the process of metamorphosis from the legends and the stories was one thing, but to witness it was another. Jake's eyes were riveted on *Shane,* who was kneeling and clasping his bony hands over his head, on which strange protuberances were piercing through with the most nauseating series of noises Jake had ever heard. *Shane* screamed in agony, and through the sobs and the yells, the following words desperately came to Jake.

"Run, J—ake. L—eave."

It was the only signal Jake needed to snap out of this utter stupor. The growling emanating from his friend was now more that of a beast. Shane was becoming less human by the minute, it seemed. Jake ran to the pickup, sat behind the steering wheel, and plucked the ignition key from behind the visor where it was hidden. Without looking back at the camp, he peeled out onto the desolate road. The screams of the thing—or the *things*—accompanied him for many miles, but never did Jake dare look around him at the source of the bestial shrieks. Once, Jake thought he glimpsed a horned shape exiting the cover of the forest. Jake put the pedal to the metal, and the thing was out of sight. Giant spruces and pines flashed by in a blur, but never did Jake slow.

A sense of safety washed over Jake when he neared Thunder Bay. He allowed himself a brief rest, to fuel the pickup and collect his wits. He now welcomed the noise and busyness of the city that he normally loathed. Jake left the gas station and entered Highway 61, never to come back.

Jake never admitted what happened that night. He only told the police and their families that they'd had the great misfortune to encounter a group of wild, rabid beasts, which Jake had miraculously escaped. Never were the bodies of Bobby, Johnny, or even Shane found. And never did Jake return to the Ruby Lake Provincial Park.

Sometimes, though, when autumn spread its colourful sheet over the world, Jake did hear the forest whispering to him,

LOCKDOWN HORROR #2

its murmurs carrying echoes of the name of a man he was desperate to see one last time.

Shane.

RAIN

By Sarah Jane Justice

She told me her name was Rain.

When she forced her fragile body into my reluctant arms, her eyes held the look of a girl who had run out of tears to cry. The hair that should have been kept in neat, ribboned pigtails fell in filthy clumps, matted across her trembling shoulders. I had promised myself that my own survival would be my sole concern, but I could never have sent Rain back into that world on her own. This was no longer a world for a child, if ever it had been.

My own limbs shook with pain and fatigue, but I forced myself to keep pulling Rain along by the hand. I wanted to guard her ears from the dull screams that hit us from behind, but they echoed down every street and dug into my sides with the force of an invisible knife. I tried not to picture the impact they would be having on someone as vulnerable as Rain, but the reflections I kept seeing in her eyes bludgeoned the reality of the matter deep into my skin.

LOCKDOWN HORROR #2

The attacker had appeared suddenly, forcing his way into our community from a background no-one could identify. He provided us with no words, no name, no justification at all to explain his actions. His presence brought only fear, to the point where reason began to look like an unnecessary afterthought. Looming over anyone who stood before him, his physical features seemed to shift away from identification. No-one who had gathered the courage to look at him directly could describe anything other than his intimidating size and shape, paired with his obvious strength. Although it was clear that he wore the body of a man, I couldn't bring myself to believe he was human. I thought of him as a creature, one who used his presence itself as a form of psychological warfare. I had never known a human being to be able to wield fear with such pointed accuracy.

We had all seen horrendous violence from the comfort of our couches. Observing the far-away aftermath of wars and bombings had led us into the false sense of assurance that we knew the look of brutality. We thought we understood it, by appearance at least. The displays that shone back at us through the protective barrier of plastic screens demonstrated the reality of pain, a sensation we would never have expected to feel through our own skin. We had seen images of the blood that spills around jagged knives. We had seen footage of the damage that could be done by hate, even when expressed through fists alone. In recorded sounds and pictures, we thought we had seen the worst our world could offer. We hadn't seen this.

Our attacker launched himself at anyone in his path, scanning screaming crowds with calm eyes that lacked the barest hint of emotion. From my position of attempted flight, I couldn't see any weapon other than fear, but fear alone couldn't explain the way he ripped death through endless panicking crowds. The specific methods of his violence blurred through our vision along with any key identifying features of his face. We could see only the impact of his actions, which left us with an even higher level of vulnerability. Without being able to visualise his weapon, we lacked the hope of finding any army that could plan well enough to bat it out of his maniacal hands.

In the wake of the first attacks, superstitions spread like wildfire. Knowing that the creature towering over us could still scarcely be seen in detail, many avoided looking too closely. As if our attacker held the blinding properties of the sun we had forgotten to notice, people cowered in their masses with averted eyes. If I had any inclination towards being a hero, I would have shouted them down with the knowledge that looking away only blinded them to his movements, making them more vulnerable than before. Even if I had possessed that level of selfless bravery, I knew it was unlikely to do anything more than place myself firmly and directly in the path of danger.

Once a victim fell within the creature's focus, any attempts at defence had so far proven useless. All it seemed to take was a hard, heavy glance from those apathetic eyes, and people were left hunched over in the grips of death. Without any sign of a physical touch, our entire community was falling helpless to a grim variety of mysterious causes. Some would fall to their knees, veins stretching to pop with the spitting boil of their own blood. Others would turn on each other as reluctant puppets, filled with a rage that couldn't be explained coursing suddenly through them against their will. With no power to fight their own unexpected anger, they began to turn on each other, involuntarily squaring off to maim the people they loved more than life itself.

Rain had been hit with a disease.

I had seen her symptoms flooding through the bodies I was now being forced to push past in the streets. Languishing souls struck with an unidentified sickness that left them to die slowly and painfully, buried in the dirt tracks of those who still had the strength to run. It was a fate that seemed far crueller than any other. The agony of these victims was drawn out through the lingering hope that their lungs had only been hit by a temporary cold or virus. They had the ability to deny the progression of their illness, while being weighed down by the underlying knowledge that their time left on Earth was now measured by an invisible hourglass that they would never be able to read.

It is often said that there is safety in numbers, but the scene laying itself out before me was quickly punching holes in that idea. As I hid behind any crumbling suburban shield I could find, I saw the struggle of those who had stayed too loyal. Any escape attempt carried out by more than an individual or pair was visibly held back by the clumsiness of their actions. In their numbers, they became easier to spot and more convenient to trap. From the first sound of a scream that reached my ears, I had sworn to remain loyal only to my own company. My survival was my number one priority, and the slim chances I had of getting away with my life became smaller with the burden of any kind of companion. I discovered my weakness in the realisation that, despite the cold air that kept grabbing me by the ankles, my heart remained warm.

Rain must have spotted me as I jumped out of hiding to avoid the sparks of a falling power line. I spent no more than a moment wondering who had left this frightened child to fend for herself, before remembering that no possible answer to that question could hold any kind of benefit. All I needed to know was that she was alone, and she had seen me as someone who might be able to help her.

Clutching her fragile sides, she scrambled through the wreckage towards me and attempted to beg. With muddy tears that splashed under eyes tainted with hurt, she could barely pull together any word that could describe what it was she wanted. The message in her eyes ensured no specific words were necessary to convey her desperation. I fought with all my strength to gather the scraps of selfishness I needed, digging into any depth of my soul that I could still reach. I pushed against the empathy that kept rising through my chest and told myself to run, to turn away from this girl and continue on my own. In all practical senses, Rain was already dead, but I might still have a chance. It was an internal battle that logic would never have been able to win. I was certain that no action on my part could save her, but I wouldn't be able to forgive myself if I didn't try.

She told me her name was Rain, and I was compelled to take her into my care.

With a sigh of frustration aimed at my own emotional weakness, I gripped her slippery hand in my own. Pulling Rain along behind me, I darted behind crumbling houses, towards alleyways that blocked our view of the distant flames. Her movements were hindered by the progressing decay that was already spreading through her veins, but I paced my steps to remain by her side. My actions pitched a constant battle against the voice screaming back at me from the core of my instincts. Every segment of my logical mind stood to attention and begged me to prioritise my own survival. Still, against my own strongest intentions, I couldn't leave Rain to die on her own. If I abandoned her, she would face the end of her days drenched in cold fear, miserable and alone in a dirty street. She was already marked for death, but the least I could do for her in her last days was to provide the barest amount of comfort, if not hope.

The screams flooding through to us from the town centre created a constant wall of sound as our backdrop, but it wasn't too long before I managed to detach from their meaning. Once I was able to dissociate enough to ignore the message the cries brought along with them, they became useful for measuring the distance between us and the attacker. I failed to fight back the relief that slipped into my heart when I noticed that backdrop losing its vocal edge. As we started nearing the town's edge, the streets around became quieter and the screams more distant.

Every corner we passed revealed hidden escape attempts that mirrored the movements of Rain and myself. Through visible blood and bruises, countless pairs of frightened souls held each other and fumbled towards the outskirts of the town. Even from the hunched and hurried glances I could throw in their direction, I could see they were all dizzy with fear, struggling with all their willpower to keep moving.

I didn't want to let myself rest, not even for a second. Staying still for any amount of time held the risk of making us both a sitting target, even if I did still have the ability to pull myself back up from a seated position. I could push past fatigue and keep forcing my aching limbs to keep carrying me, but Rain's limited strength was visibly leaving her body with every step. I still couldn't find it within myself to leave her, so I found a corner sheltered enough to give us the slightest chance of remaining unseen. She slumped against my side and I pulled her close into a huddle, trying to ignore the sickly colour that was beginning to spread in patches across her skin. Unwilling to make any noise I could avoid, I attempted to use my eyes to convey the silent message that everything was going to be ok. I knew there was no chance left of that, but I wanted Rain to believe it. Her barely responsive nod told me that she was trying her best, but I could see that she had already lost her capacity for belief. Forcing myself to look away from the dying child in my arms, I tried to focus on the screams.

With a lurch that hit me in the stomach like a cannonball, my ears caught a wailing cry that pierced the air out of nowhere. The distant screams had been continuing to fade, but this one had come from very nearby. One by one, similar sounds began to flood into the space around me, spreading like a heavy fog into my ears. Clutching my terrified palms into white-knuckled fists, I felt myself forget how to breathe.

The implication of defeat left me wanting to curl into a ball against the bricks that were holding me up, but I pushed past it to steady what little breath I could muster. I needed to keep fighting, and for that to be possible, I needed to see what was happening. Forcing a reluctant gasp of stale air back into my lungs, I craned my neck towards the sounds.

SISSY FUSS

By Shawn M. Klimek

Kinter clung to the mountain, injured and shivering. His partner dangled unconscious from a belaying cord cinched to his hip. The wind tugged at it, hammering his sore back and frostbitten digits. Every plume of fog exiting his nostrils meant more warmth escaping. "I'm in Hell," he moaned into another icy blast.

Suddenly…hope!

His lost pocketknife glinted on the rocks below.

Reaching for it, he fumbled, then slipped and plummeted.

Somehow recovered but scraped raw, he clung desperately to the icy rocks.

Something glinted just out of reach.

His lost knife!

Oh right, he remembered. *I'm literally in Hell.*

A RECOVERED LETTER

By Horatio Marissa

Transcription of the last known letter correspondence between Dr. William T. Clay and Dr. Alfred McMillian. Sent from Bramwell, West Virginia, to New York City,

New York. Letter dated November 17th, 1893.

Dear Alfred,

I hope, dearly, that this letter finds you quickly. I fear my case in Mercer County has taken a turn for the worst, and I require immediate assistance from you. Stating it in such a manner seems like a massive underestimation, but there it is. I'll be blunt: in my ten years of practice, I've never before witnessed something of this manner. To prepare you, I'll detail the events of the past few days below. I fear you'll think ill of me after I am done, or that I've gone mad, but I assure you that I am in as sound a mind as ever.

I arrived at the Latimer residence on

LOCKDOWN HORROR #2

November 15th. It's some five miles from Bramwell, a small mining community, and I walked the distance, as I couldn't find a soul heading the same direction. I was asked to come, as you may recall, by an old friend of mine, Ernest Latimer. We met when I still took regular calls to the country, and we've been fast friends since. I even attended his wedding. His wife, Libbie, was the patient in question. She was born and raised on a tiny settlement, deep in the Appalachian woods—its name escapes me—and though she is kind enough, there's always been an odd air to her. She visits home regularly. It was on one of these trips—and this part is so odd that I asked twice for clarification from Ernest—that she was attacked by a deer.

I'm aware that you were raised in the city, Alfred, and I therefore offer that deer attacks are nearly unheard of. They're flighty creatures, who will startle at the slightest movement. Nevertheless, a vicious bite wound does, or did, reside on Libbie's forearm. The teeth marks would indicate that the attacker was, in fact, a deer, though the wound was very ragged.

After arriving back home on November 8th, Libbie began to complain of feeling feverish, and Ernest noticed she was visibly flushed. Her fever refused to break after three nights, and after discovering the wound to be inflamed, I was called.

I remember that, upon stepping into the house, I was struck with an odd smell.

It was sweet, unpleasantly so, but so low-lying that it could have been an odd fruit, or a meal left in the cupboard too long. As we walked through the house, the smell grew stronger, until it was actively distracting once we reached the bedroom. I am well acquainted with the smell of sickness, Alfred, and though the two were close enough that one could be compared to the other, they were distinctly different. Ernest slowly opened the door, and I stepped inside.

Libbie was awake and lucid when I first examined her, if a bit fatigued. I sat by her and had her explain the encounter once again. Though nothing in our conversation seemed amiss at the time, looking back, she reacted quite oddly to some of my questions. When asked if a deer had bitten her, she took a long moment to answer. Her face contorted slightly as she nodded, as though she wasn't quite sure. She also complained of a bad headache, which I attributed to the fever. I feel like a fool now for doing so, but as I retrace my steps through the encounter, I find that my first assertion was logical. There was simply no way of knowing. I will go on, Alfred. You must excuse these guilty ramblings of mine. I am in a bad way after tonight's transpirings.

The deer bite worried me; the veins that lead away from it had taken up a swollen, red complexion that was characteristic of infection. I washed the wound and applied a topical rub, before rebandaging it, and bid Libbie rest. Ernest allowed me to sleep in their spare bedroom, which next to Libbie's bedroom, and the odd smell seemed to permeate through the wall. I found myself so irritated that, when alone, I took to hooking my shirt up over my nose to block out the scent. My sleep was fitful and when I woke the next morning, I was sore and tired.

Libbie's condition had only worsened in the night. I ate, before examining her once more. The smell in the room was now so strong that I coughed upon opening the door. Her face only looked more flushed, but there was a certain gauntness to it that I hadn't seen before. She complained once again of a headache, and told me that she was dreadfully hungry. None of the inflammation in the wound had gone away. After she had eaten, I let two pints of blood from her, before bidding her sleep again. She did so with little hesitation.

Ernest and I spent much of the day in the house. There were a whole host of chores to be done now that Libbie was sick, so we spent much of our time fetching wood for the fireplace, tidying the rooms we had disrupted, and cooking. Libbie slept fitfully, and more than once woke in a desperate state of thirst. I would bring her a glass of water, which she would quickly drain. The fourth time this happened, she brought the glass to her lips, before suddenly convulsing, and vomiting across the bed sheets. I tried to see this as a good sign, as the body expelling bad matter, but as Ernest and I attempted to change the bedsheets, this line of thinking was quickly abandoned. Among the bile and food lay several clumps of hair. It was very short hair—like the trimmings of a beard—and dark brown. I was dumbfounded, and determined to set my mind to other matters as I washed the blankets. Even so, I couldn't help but notice how Libbie's vomit seemed to radiate the same sickly-sweet smell that filled the house. Even now, the scent lingers on my hands, caked into my nail beds, hiding in the crevices of my palms. I long to bathe.

Libbie fell back asleep after Ernest replaced her sheets. By this time it was nearing dark, and my old friend practically fell into his chair by the fireplace, exhaustion plain across his face. We spoke in hushed tones to pass the time. Though we attempted not to touch the matter at hand, it was clear that he was deeply concerned with his wife's health. His eye would drift to the door of their bedroom anytime there was a lull in the conversation, and though I tried to distract him with talk, there was a distant look in his eye that never left through our whole conversation. An hour or so must have passed before the fire reduced in size such that we could barely see. Ernest made to rise, but I assured him I could fetch the firewood, and I left the house for the shed, where the logs are stacked. As the last of the days light faded from the sky, I couldn't help but stare out at the mountains. During the day, the Appalachian Mountains are strikingly beautiful, and in the night this effect is not lost, but it is distinctly not the same. In darkness, the mountains seem somehow larger, and their stillness is almost eerie. For a moment, they struck me nor as mountains, but as a giant creature, unmoving but alive, observing me from above. And in that moment, I was very afraid.

When I entered the house once more, Ernest was gone from his seat. It shouldn't have struck me as odd, but an odd sense of dread had followed me in from outside, and I abruptly set the firewood down and observed the room. Quickly, I came to the realization that the door to the bedroom was open. I lit a candle and came inside.

Libbie was asleep, and Ernest stood over her. I whispered his name, but there was no response from him. It was in that moment that I realised that he was shaking violently, like he'd caught a continual chill. My attention snapped back to Libbie, but she was breathing. The warm light of the candle glistened when it met her skin. She was so slick with sweat that she looked as if she had been doused in water. This detail had captured me so that I didn't notice it until Ernest gave a shuddering gasp and finally spoke. "William," he said, his voice tight and quavering, "look at the top of her head."

I did so, and froze.

At first, I thought it was some sort of worm. Somehow, I thought, a very large worm had made its way into the room and had latched itself onto Libbie's scalp. But that wasn't right. The thing was too long, too thick, too like a muscle to be anything but animal. As I stared, my mind reeling, I began to notice the small bits of gore hung from her hair and dripped onto the pillow. Whatever it was wasn't latched onto her, I realised. Something inside her skull had punctured its way through the roof of her skull. It was impossible, but there it was. Slowly, I stared down at Libbie. She was serene in her sleep, and still breathing slowly. This, somehow, made my horror grow, as I turned back to the wound, and the alien object suddenly came into sharp focus.

It wasn't a worm. It was the tail of a

rat.

As if to confirm my theory, the thing twitched suddenly. Ernest stumbled backward and fell, but I remained rooted to the spot, transfixed by the impossible sight.

Upon the sound of her husband's fall, Libbie's eyes opened. Both Ernest and I froze as she sleepily surveyed the room. "William," she said slowly.

"Hello, Libbie," I heard myself saying slowly. "How do you feel?"

She smiled, and there was a short brown hair stuck between two of her teeth. "I feel much better," she said. Her words slurred slightly, as if she'd had too much to drink. I realised with a start that I was backing slowly away from her.

"Is something wrong?" she asked.

Sweat was pouring down her forehead in sheets down, and she blinked lazily as it spilled into her open eyes.

Then, suddenly, the strip of skin from her collarbone to her back bulged.

My first thought, as I turned and ran from the room, was that she'd had a massive muscle spasm. I knew better, though; Muscles spasms don't move like that at all. It was far too large, and in a place where there was little tissue. The sight repeated in my mind as I fell against Ernest's chair by the fire. The husband was soon after me, and we cowered away from the door to the bedroom, which we dared not go back to close.

There was the sound of fabric shifting, and a soft thump as Libbie's feet hit the floor. "Libbie," I called, "you're very sick. Go back to bed." She ignored me, instead emerging slowly from the doorway. Her walk was odd, accented by jerks and spasms of muscle. Ernest stood, paralyzed, beside me. We both watched in rapt horror as she stumbled toward us. Her nightgown lay close to her skin, and I could see the fabric ripple oddly around her, as though there was something small and quick running about under it. If there was, she showed no signs of discomfort.

"Ernest," she said placidly, "I feel a lot better now."

Ernest slowly moved to pass me, but I held my arm out, stopping him. Libbie frowned. "Ernest," she said, but her voice was wrong when she said it, too strained, too low. "Ernest." Then, she gave a soft groan as her mouth fell open limply. I suspect that her jaw muscles had been chewed through at that point, for her mouth hung far too wide open. She seemed to want to try and speak, but all that came out was a wet choking sound. She didn't seem to notice this. She didn't even seem to notice when the thing in her throat finished crawling out.

It perched in her unhinged jaw, staring forward expectantly. It was a fat, brown rat. Its coat had been dyed dark with something I couldn't make out, but its small pale hands were slick with blood. The thing leapt from her jaw onto the front of her nightgown, before skittering to the ground. It ran toward us, and Ernest screamed, kicking it away. It landed in a heap by the fireplace.

Libbie moaned loudly, and suddenly two more rats had replaced the first. Then another. And another. Her arms and legs seized with activity, writhing in a manner more akin to a snake than a human limb. The rats began to pour steadily from her mouth, her flesh stretching and tearing, until her cheeks were reduced to a mess of torn flesh. As they poured out, Libbie seemed to shrink slightly as the rats fled her, a motion I can only liken to a sandcastle crumbling when water is poured atop it.

In this moment, something in Ernest seemed to snap, and with a tortured cry, he ran forward, and pushed what remained of his wife down the cellar stairs. As she fell, her form contorted, and for a single second I thought faintly that her form was more like a bag made of skin anything remotely human. Then Ernest slammed the door.

As I write you, my back is pressed to that very same door. It's been around five hours since what happened, happened. The smell is unbearable, even after Ernest and I shoved blankets in the crack under the door. Ernest has been in and out of the room, seemingly determined to capture every last rat in the house. There has been no noise from Libbie, but I find myself imagining her standing just outside the door, listening to me labour away at this letter.

I can still hear the rats, though. They

skitter across the floor of the cellar, scratch at the stairs, gnaw at the door. I dare not leave my post.

Come quickly.

Yours,

Will Clay

LEFT HANGING

By Beth W. Patterson

We were drawn to this location because, like us, it was once alive: fire and molten rock, thought and enlightenment flowing, ash soaring, reaching from hell to the heavens. But with the cooling comes the dying, unchanging, and forgetting.

Dead entities gain their energy from the living. The outcropping offered us some measure of wordless sympathy, but we still longed for our lost abilities to think. All things must persevere, and Saint Valentine's Day was a lovely day for a picnic. The brains of the young ladies seeking knowledge tasted sweet.

For our crimes, we became one with the stones.

ISOLATION

By D.M. Burdett

Breathe in. Breathe out.

***

The peak hour train was heaving;

sweaty bodies crowded in against one another in the small space.

Jacob squeezed himself into a corner and pushed in his earphones, turning up the volume to block out the noise. He faced the wall, his eyes closed, and studiously ignored the penned in feeling that threatened his fragile anxiety.

Breathe in. Breathe out.

He hated them all. All the people with their made-up faces, their perfect hair, their shaggy beards, their beautiful suits, their purposeful lives. He hated every one of them.

Someone knocked into him, and Jacob twitched at the touch as a twang of fear flashed through his body. His eyes sprung open and he started to hyperventilate, his heart thudding in his ears.

Don't touch me! Don't touch me!

But the man settled back against the wall, hands in pockets, his body jiggling rhythmically with the train's movements.

Jacob closed his eyes once more.

***

"Good morning, Jacob." Cindy, the receptionist, smiled at him as he passed through the building's entrance atrium.

Don't speak to me! Don't speak to me!

"Morning," Jacob muttered as he hastened to the elevators.

In the enclosed space of his tiny cubicle, Jacob finally relaxed, comforted by the familiarity of the space and the closeness of the walls. He stripped off his coat and hung it on the peg before pulling a flask from his backpack and pouring a coffee. The communal kitchen was not a place that he would ever frequent.

He flicked on his computer screen and began his solitary tasks.

***

"Alright, Jakey?" Bill, the weird IT bloke, leaned his elbows on the partition and peered over.

Jacob grimaced internally at the invasion but smiled weakly.

No, no, no, no, no.

"Do anything good over the weekend?"

Jacob shook his head tentatively, not taking his eyes from the computer screen.

Almost bobbing up and down, Bill was desperate to share his weekend's exploits. "Well." Bill's eyes darted furtively around the open office. "I hacked the dark web!" he whispered excitedly.

Jacob raised his head slightly with a disinterested, but polite, raise of his eyebrows, but carried on working through his computer-generated workload.

"Yeah, man. Some weird shit on there," Bill said with a laugh. "There's fucking freaky people in the world!"

Jacob gave a wan smile, but didn't make eye contact. The rising panic had already contracted the muscles in his neck, and his heart was pounding painfully.

Go away. Go away.

"Some shit that'll make you want to bleach your eyes and lay down with a shotgun for a soother." Bill looked shiftily around the room again, then back at Jacob. He watched for a few moments as Jacob carried on typing.

"You can buy the passwords to 50 million bank accounts for 50 bucks," he enthused. "Hire a hit man. There's a social media app that connects you with people who think they're vampires and want to buy your blood. And I even saw a chick on there who wants to be killed."

Jacob's fingers paused on the keyboard, aware of Bill's eyes on him, but the pause seemed to indicate interest to Bill.

"Yeah, yeah! She's *actually* looking for someone to kill her. Dumb-ass broad. Her post says she wants to know what's it's like to die." Bill disappeared from the top of the partition and reappeared in the doorway of the cubicle.

Jacob frowned at the invasion.

Go away. Go away.

"She wants money in exchange. There's an auction. Nuts, huh?"

Jacob concentrated on his breathing.

Breathe in. Breathe out.

"I wonder what a dead girl needs money for." Bill pondered his own question with a furrowed brow, but then shrugged. "People are fucking nuts, man."

After a moment, Jacob began typing again, and eventually Bill wandered out of the cubicle to find someone else to bug.

***

Jacob left the office late, and so there were fewer people at the train terminal. He climbed into a coach that was deserted other than a young woman who sat at the opposite end, earphones plugged in. Just how he liked it.

There was no-one who would touch him, ooze their smells his way, speak to him.

Breathe in. Breathe out.

Even so, he arrived home exhausted, flinging his bag on the floor before rifling through the freezer for a microwave meal.

As the microwave hummed in the

background, Jacob opened his laptop and logged into the darknet browser, navigating to the website where he'd placed his ad.

YOU HAVE 1 MESSAGE

The microwave beeped, and he slopped a grey meal onto a plate before pulling a stool up to the counter. He scooped up a forkful of bland nutrients as his finger swiped across the mousepad to open the message.

The fork stopped halfway to his lips; it was a reply to his advert.

His heart fluttered; SadMan62 wanted to transact.

He dropped the still-laden fork back onto the plate and pulled the laptop closer.

He opened up the advert that he'd placed, rechecking the text to assure himself that he'd been clear in his request.

'I want to experience the kill, feel the life drain away.'

He had hoped this might quell his fear of human contact—to be able to touch another's flesh in their final breaths without fear of their rejection, or of his repulsion causing offense.

He hunched over his keyboard and sent a speedy reply.

***

Jacob felt alive and excited, even though he'd hardly slept a wink all night. He pulled back the bedcovers and sat up, switching off the alarm clock a long while before it was due to go off.

In the kitchen, he made a cup of coffee. He realised he was humming—a tuneless melody—and marvelled at the sound.

Is this what it's like to feel happy?

He padded to the lounge with his cup and surveyed the preparations he'd made the night before. He'd followed SadMan62's instructions meticulously; the room was encased in plastic sheeting, taped to the walls and over all the furniture.

Jacob could hardly contain the elation, his hope for the future, that this encounter would free him from his lifelong anxieties.

A knife sat on the coffee table, alongside an unopened bottle of gin.

A knife to the jugular. Quick and easy,

SadMan62 had said.

Jacob went back to the kitchen and dropped his cup in the sink before returning to the bedroom to shower and dress.

***

Jacob sat on the edge of the chair, elbows on knees and his hands rubbing around each other, a bead of sweat trickling down his forehead—excitement mixed with nerves—staring at the items on the coffee table. He straightened the knife for the hundredth time.

He twitched when the doorbell rang.

Breathe in. Breathe out.

He stood up quickly, knocking the coffee table, and the knife scuttered to the floor. He picked it up and placed it reverently back next to the gin.

He wanted everything to be just right. He owed it to SadMan62. For his sacrifice.

He hurried to the door and took a deep, ragged breath before opening it.

Breathe in. Breathe out.

"Alright, Jakey," Bill Pheal, the weird IT guy, stepped into Jacob's hallway and closed the door behind him.

"Wha— You're…you're…" Jacob stuttered.

"Yeah, I'm SadMan," Bill grinned. "Did you make everything like we talked about," he said, suddenly sombre.

Jacob nodded absently, still reeling. "Through there," he said, pointing to the lounge.

Bill looked around at the small, plastic-coated room. "Wow! You really did a great job." His eyes settled on the knife, and he sank down onto the sofa. "That's the knife then," he said, softly.

Jacob sat down next to Bill, and they both gazed at the sharp instrument. "Yeah," he breathed, "that's the knife."

The two men sat in silence for an eternity before Bill reached for the gin and poured out two large measures.

"Fuck," he said, handing a glass to Jacob. "This is harder than I thought it was going to be."

Both men gulped their drinks down in one mouthful.

"OK." Bill turned slightly in his seat, so for the first time he looked into Jacob's eyes. "Shall we get on with it?"

Jacob nodded and, after a moment's hesitation, reached for the knife with trembling fingers.

But Bill beat him to it.

Jacob looked from the twinkling point of the blade to Bill's grin, and back again.

"But…" Jacob stuttered.

"What?" Bill asked, feigning innocence.

"We…we had an agreement. The knife is for me."

"The knife *is* for you, Jakey. You want to 'feel the kill'."

Bill plunged the knife into Jacob's neck.

"You want to feel the life drain away, Jakey-boy." He pushed Jacob onto his back as he writhed and bucked.

"Are you feeling the kill, Jakey? Do you feel it?" he breathed into Jacob's twitching face.

"You got what you wanted, Jakey. Now I'll get what I want," he said, holding Jacob's face in one hand and twisting his head.

"Did you see my advert, Jakey? Did you see it?"

Bill pressed his lips to the jagged cut and gulped the thick, pumping liquid.

Breathe out.

BUS TRIP

By Stephen Herczeg

As the great silver bus stood, waiting to take him home for the holidays, David wished he could fly back to Adelaide, but his mother put all her money into sending him to University and could only afford bus fare. Besides, it was either the bus trip home or spending Christmas in Canberra, which even the permanent residents abandoned at that time of year.

David climbed aboard and found a vacant row half way along the bus. Far enough away from the toilet at the rear to avoid the smell and far enough from the driver in case he got too chatty. He favoured the window seat as it offered the extra stimulation of viewing the countryside passing by, though most of the trip would be through the desolate wastelands of the Hay plains.

He plonked down and pulled out his book for the journey. He read the title— *Fourier series of the Periodic Bernoulli and Euler Functions*—and sighed. A sixteen-hour bus trip and the dynamic world of applied mathematics to keep him company.

Movement in the aisle dragged his attention away from his riveting read. He looked up into a pair of sparkling blue eyes framed in long blonde hair.

"David isn't it?" the owner of the eyes asked.

David immediately recognised the owner as Hannah, a fellow student from his chemistry class. Her eyes passed over his book and a smile came to her lips.

"Nice book. Applied Maths three next year, right?" she asked.

David nodded.

"Yep. With Professor Chan. Meant to be tough, so I thought I'd bone up before term starts. Also thought it would put me to sleep pretty damn quick," he said.

Hannah laughed. She indicated the seat next to David. "Is this taken?"

"Not at all," he said. "Hang on." He rose and shuffled out from the window seat. "You can have the window. I think my book will provide enough stimulation for my tired mind."

"Thanks," she said.

Hannah edged into the window seat. David sat down, and they began to talk. Surprisingly, they had lived close to each other for the best part of their short lives. The only reasons they had never met were caused by the instituted feeding boundaries for South Australian high schools. Their parents' houses were on opposite sides of the boundary, forcing them to attend different schools.

Because of that, Hannah's parents had found the money to send her to an exclusive private girls' school rather than attend the state school. Her grades had been so good that she'd qualified for a scholarship and ended up at the Australian National University, along with David.

They talked for what seemed like half an hour, but when they pulled into the Gundagai roadhouse, they both realised it had been closer to two hours. Hannah smiled as the buildings near the *Dog on the Tucker Box* came into sight.

"I need to stretch my legs," she said.

They both moved outside and grabbed what passed as a coffee in the roadhouse.

Between gulps of the steaming hot liquid, they continued their conversation, and David took a chance. He suggested they share a cab when they reached the bus station in Adelaide. Hannah agreed with a wistful smile on her lips and playfully moved a lock of her long blonde hair away from her face and behind her ear.

She excused herself and moved off to the bathrooms, peering back towards David before moving into the building.

David's chest only managed to hold on to his swiftly beating heart through sheer willpower. There was something here. With Hannah. It was only a spark, but it could be the start of something huge in his life.

Back on the bus, their conversation

eventually lulled into silence. David's attention turned to his textbook, while Hannah made a pillow out of her jumper and curled up for a nap. The paragraphs of dense text and complicated formulae before David's eyes blurred into the scribblings of a three-year-old. All he could see, in his mind's eye, was that smile, those eyes and that lock of hair.

His eyes darted to his right from time to time, in a vain attempt to catch a glimpse of Hannah's face, her eyes, or anything really.

Finally, the textbook took its toll and his eyelids drooped and closed, sending him into dreamland where images of Hannah swirled amongst the lines of mathematical equations—equations that formed a timeline of possibilities that ended with he and Hannah in a dreamland paradise for the rest of their lives.

***

David awoke with a start and checked his watch. Four hours had passed since the bus left Gundagai. He looked through the window.

Outside, wide-open plains covered in brown grass stretched off to the horizon that consisted of mile after mile of rolling brown hills. A river wound its way through the hills, its banks home to small copses of green tipped eucalypts. It was stark, but in a beautiful way.

Yep, we could be anywhere.

His eyes dropped to Hannah. She was asleep as well. Her head lolled against the window, jiggling with the movement of the bus. He peered around to check if anyone was watching, then turned his attention back to her. He stared and admired the lines of her face, her high cheekbones, her long lashes and flowing flaxen hair.

She's so beautiful. She'd never go for a dope like me. But there is something there. She smiled. And she wants to share a cab.

He checked the rest of the bus again. Everybody else seemed to be asleep as well. Even to someone who had taken this trip so many times that seemed odd. Usually there was some movement. The tinny sound of music coming from a pair of headphones. The hum of idle chatter. Something. But the only sounds he heard were the road noise rising through the floor and the only movement was the scenery flashing by outside.

He turned his gaze back to Hannah. His eyes traced every curve and line on her face. He glanced down further for a moment, but his timidity with women forced his attention back to her face. That's when he noticed it.

He craned forward for a better look.

Hannah had a small white blemish beneath her left eye. David moved in closer and examined the discolouration. He found it mildly exciting that someone so flawless had an imperfection.

Suddenly, the small white patch

moved.

David flinched, the heavy textbook slipped off his lap and thumped to the floor.

"Bugger," he said out loud.

He looked down and tried to reach for the book. His outstretched fingers brushed the edge and accidentally pushed it further away. He reached further, but the book refused to be captured. Suddenly, his shoulder flared in pain as it cramped up. He pulled away and sat up, his free hand going to his aching shoulder.

"Ah, crap," he said, rubbing at the knot in his shoulder muscle. After a couple of agonising minutes, the muscles finally relaxed, and the pain subsided. He glanced across at Hannah to see if he'd woken her.

His mouth dropped open and his eyes

grew wide in shock. The pain in his shoulder was forgotten immediately, and he leaned in for a closer look.

The skin beneath Hannah's eye pulsated as if alive with a will of its own.

"Hannah?" David said, and reached out for her shoulder.

Suddenly, the skin burst open and a small white creature with a black head wriggled out of the hole. David reeled back in abject horror. His foot shot out and kicked the book further down towards the front of the bus.

He stared back at the thing on Hannah's face.

A maggot.

David gagged at the sight. His hand went to his mouth to quell an ejection of vomit. He watched fascinated as the maggot wiggled across Hannah's cheek and slipped off into her hair.

He reached out with his other hand and gave the sleeping girl a slight nudge.

"Hannah?" he asked again. She stayed still. The maggot the only movement.

David's fear grew.

She's dead.

He reached out, grabbed her shoulder and shook. He wanted to wake her up, to make sure she was still alive. She stayed still, scaring him even more. In his panic, he shook harder.

Suddenly, her skin ripped open from cheek to neck. Blood and maggots poured from the wound and spilled across her chest.

David jumped out of his seat and gaped back. Revulsion stirred his stomach, and terror filled his mind. The woman that mere hours ago was so full of life and beauty, now sat split open amidst a teeming mass of maggots.

"Hannah?" he cried. His stomach convulsed and let fly. He filled his now vacant seat with his lunch, breakfast and last night's dinner. The vile smelling liquid splashing across the seething mass that was now Hannah. He coughed, spitting the final dregs into his seat and stood up.

Hannah's chest and lap were now a sea of writhing white maggots bathed in Hannah's red lifeblood. As he watched, her body deflated and began to slip off the seat.

In a panic, he turned and grabbed the

arm of the reclining man next to him. He shook the man to try to wake him.

"Sir, please help, sir," he shouted staring back as Hannah's body collapsed in on itself.

The man continued to doze.

David shook harder. His plea was met with a sharp crack as the man's arm tore away from his shoulder. Blood sprayed from the wound, bathing David's pants in a fine red shower. David screamed and dropped the arm. It flopped to the floor at his feet.

He looked at the man's face. The skin started peeling away in ragged clumps of red, revealing the meat and bone beneath. More maggots pushed out of the muscles and crawled across the open flesh.

David simply stared open mouthed for a moment. He gagged in revulsion, but there was nothing left to bring up.

He backed away down the aisle. All thoughts of his book and of Hannah banished from his mind. He needed safety. He needed to retreat from the blood-soaked nightmare before him. He glanced at the passengers on either side. And screamed again.

All four people were disintegrating into pools of accelerated decay. Their facial skin sloughing off and falling into their laps amidst a waterfall of blood and mucus as he stepped past.

David turned and raced towards the driver. He concentrated and blinkered his vision to avoid glancing at the devastated bodies of the other passengers on either side, but glimpses of putrescence seeped into his peripheral vision. He gulped, put his head down and proceeded to the front.

David hunkered down besides the driver's seat. Behind the Perspex screen, the driver ignored him and continued to stare at the road ahead. David tapped on the plastic and tried to sound calm, so he could be understood.

"Hey, Sir," David said, "there's people back there. Dead people. You need to do something."

The driver's face remained fixed, staring straight ahead. David rapped harder and raised his voice.

"Sir, they are dead and..."—he stifled a cry of hysteria—"...rotting, Sir."

The driver continued to ignore him. David's terror gave way to anger. He made a fist and pounded on the window.

"Hey," he shouted and finally got a reaction. The driver's head slowly turned towards him. David fell backwards in horror. The driver's face was missing, replaced by white bone and empty eye sockets. Small flaps of red-tinged skin and muscle hung from the bone. Trails of red dribbled down the man's remaining face. David caught a glimpse of the facial meat resting in the driver's lap and threatening to drop under the buses' pedals.

"Oh my God," David gulped.

He got to his feet, turned and grabbed the entrance door handle.

"Let me out."

He shook the handle with all his might. Nothing. He screamed and hit the door in anger with the palm of his hand.

He turned around. The driver was still looking at him; his rictus grin chilled David to the bone. Slowly, the driver's head turned back to face the road. David followed his stare. The open countryside rolled towards them in endless waves of brown dirt and grass.

At least outside it's still normal.

David looked up the aisle towards the rear window.

I gotta get out.

He took off and stumbled towards the back of the bus. He kept his eyes directed at the rear, ignoring the dead bodies on either side. He tripped on something and fell forward. His hand landed on the dismembered arm, eliciting a slight scream from his ravaged throat. He pushed the arm aside and looked back at his feet.

His stupid textbook lay several feet away where it had come to rest after he'd tripped on it.

Damn maths.

He got to his feet and saw movement towards the back of the bus. A man was moving towards the toilet.

Someone else. Someone like me.

"Hey, Sir," shouted David. He lurched towards the man, almost losing his feet as the bus rocked and rolled. David reached a hand out towards the man's shoulder. The bus bucked and threw him off balance. His hand landed in the middle of the man's back, pitching them both forwards.

A loud crack reverberated over the road noise. The man's head bent backwards and flopped against his back. A pair of accusing eyes stared into David's for a moment before the last pieces of gristle snapped and the head dropped to the floor and rolled towards him. He jumped back in terror. The eyes remained fixed on his with an unblinking stare for a moment, then the skin let go and peeled away, revealing more bone and meat. The man's body teetered for a moment, then fell forward with a resounding thump.

Tears streamed down David's face as his confused brain tried to process everything. He looked up from the decapitated man and focused on the rear window. As with all modern buses, it was the emergency exit.

He made his way past the remaining seats. Mercifully they were empty with no further atrocities to greet him.

He looked at the window. The handles to pull the window out were on the exterior to aid emergency workers. A small note said: In case of emergency kick glass out.

David sidled up, kicked with all his might and bounced backwards. The window stubbornly stayed fixed in place. He steadied himself and managed to land a stronger kick. The window bucked and shifted a little. He smiled and stepped back a few paces. He turned, dropped his shoulder and ran forward as fast as he could. As luck would have it, the bus rocked at the same moment adding momentum to David's run.

He hit the window with such force that both he and it exploded from the bus.

The wind burst from his lungs as he hit the road. A crack in his shoulder was met with a flash of pain that streaked through his mind. He rolled several times before coming to a stop and gingerly got to his knees. The bus continued down the road, throwing up a plume of dust as if he'd never been aboard.

David peered around at the barren landscape. Another streak of pain hit; he winced in agony and put a hand to his injured shoulder. He tried to work out where he was and figured he was somewhere between Narrandera and Hay.

His shoulders slumped at the prospect of up to a hundred kilometres of road standing between him and the nearest town.

He turned and began walking towards the setting sun.

The sound of a car made him turn and gingerly hold out a thumb. An older model Falcon crested a nearby rise and approached him. He shook his thumb and looked hopefully at the driver. They made brief eye contact and the car pulled over. David staggered to the car and got into the rear seat.

An elderly couple looked over the front seats at him with bright smiles on their faces.

"Gidday, I'm Tony and this is my wife Jan," said the driver. His face turned to a look of concern. "Haven't seen any cars for miles, so what the hell are you doing out here on your own, young feller?" he asked.

David coughed and replied, "I fell out of a bus."

The couple laughed.

"Good one," said Tony. He turned around and said, over his shoulder, "well buckle up, we're stopping in Hay in about an hour. Get comfortable. Hope you like fifties music cause that's all we have."

He pulled out onto the highway and started to drive. David quickly buckled his seatbelt. Elvis began to come out of the car's speakers.

David sat back, stared out the window at the landscape passing by and tried to take it all in. To his fevered mind, the day was too insane to be real. Maybe it wasn't. Maybe it was all just a dream. Maybe he was still dreaming. Maybe he had fallen out of the bus. Maybe Hannah was okay. Maybe there was hope that he could find her again. Maybe he could find an explanation and beg for some sort of forgiveness.

He sighed deeply and focused on the two people in the front. Jan's head was just a ball of dark hair, but Tony was bald, and the shining skin showed through the hole in the headrest.

David noticed a small patch of white skin on the back of Tony's head. His eyes grew wide. He leaned forward and studied the back of the driver's head.

He'd seen a white spot like it not long

ago. Below the eye of his new-found love.

Suddenly, it moved.

David screamed.

First published in *Beginnings*, Australian Speculative Fiction Group, 2018

GRAVE CONCERNS

By Zoey Xolton

The graveyard was silent and still as dusk descended. The moment the sun sank beneath the hills—freshly dug earth and solid ground alike—stirred, and rasping voices rose. Pale hands burst through the soil, reaching skyward, sunken flesh clawing its way out of the grave.

The groundsman reloaded his shotgun, sheathed knives, and holstered his hatchet. He was getting on, and this game was growing old.

His apprentice, Jason, stood wide-eyed—frozen. "Rachel?" he whispered.

The groundsman took aim… Moments later Rachel's decayed brains painted a nearby tree.

Jason's pained howl of anguish joined the cacophony of the living undead.

First published *100 Word Horrors – 4*, KJK Publishing, 2019

LOCKDOWN HORROR #2

ABOUT THE PUBLISHER

BLACK HARE PRESS is a small, independent publisher based in Melbourne, Australia.

Founded in 2018, our aim has always been to champion emerging authors from all around the globe and offer opportunities for them to participate in speculative fiction and horror short story anthologies.

Connect

Website: *www.blackharepress.com*

Twitter: *@BlackHarePress*

LOCKDOWN HORROR #2

LOCKDOWN HORROR #2